koyal dark, mango sweet

KASHMIRA SHETH

HYPERION
NEW YORK

This book is a work of fiction. Names, characters, places, and incidents are either the product of the author's imagination or are used fictitiously. Any resemblance to actual events or locales or persons, living or dead, is coincidental.

For information address Hyperion Books for Children, 114 Fifth Avenue, New York, New York 10011-5690.
First Edition
1 3 5 7 9 10 8 6 4 2
Printed in the United States of America
This book is set in 12-point Kennerley.
Reinforced binding

Library of Congress Cataloging-in-Publication Data
Sheth, Kashmira.
Koyal dark, mango sweet/Kashmira Sheth.—1st ed.
p. cm.
Summary: Growing up with her family in Mumbai, India, sixteen-year-old Jeeta disagrees with much of her mother's traditional advice about how to live her life and tries to be more modern and independent.
ISBN 0-7868-3857-4
[India—Fiction. 2. Family life—India—Fiction. 3. East Indians—Fiction. 4. Interpersonal relations—Fiction.] I. Title.
PZ7.S5543Koy 2006
[Fic]—dc22 2005050338
Visit www.hyperionteens.com

For my daughters, Neha and Rupa

My heartfelt thanks to the following people for their help:

Members of my writing groups:

Write On and Tuesdays with Story.

The team at Hyperion.

And especially, Donna Bray, Vita Dani, Shilpa Dave, Arianne Lewin, Marjorie Melby, Corey Meyer, Chris Paskus, Vinitha Pittala, Charlotte Sheedy, Neha Sheth, Rajan Sheth, Samir Sheth, Amit Trivedi, Bharatiben Trivedi, Joey Valdez, and Rupa Valdez.

one

MUMMY KNOCKED on the door. "Jeeta, enough *thaga-thiya.* If you don't come out this minute you'll have to stay in there for two hours."

Every time a prospective groom came to see my twenty-one-year-old sister, Nimita, Mummy asked my other sister, Mohini, and me to disappear into the streets of Mumbai. Mummy told us it was because Nimita and the boy needed time to be alone. Sure—as alone as bees are in their hives. The boy usually came with three or four relatives, so what difference did it make if Mohini and I were there or not? Maybe it was because Mohini was nineteen and I was sixteen, and the poor boy would get confused between us all.

Mummy knocked again. "JEETA!"

"Will you really make me stay in here for two hours? What if someone needs to use the bathroom?" I said as I came out.

Mummy strode to the door of our apartment and held it open. Mohini was waiting outside at the top of the staircase.

"Go, go, hurry, the guests will be here any minute." Mummy motioned with her arm as if to sweep me out.

"I can't go barefoot. Let me at least slip on my sandals."

"Stay out for a while."

"We will," Mohini said as we went down the stairs.

Mummy shut the door.

"You escaped before Mummy got mad," Mohini said.

"Yup! Did you see the way Mummy flicked me out of the house as if I were a bedbug? I wiggled away before she stomped and squashed me, though. I'm quick."

"Not always. What took you so long to get ready?"

"Why does it matter? We're out of the house, aren't we? I don't enjoy being kicked out. I hope this boy is the caboose. You know, the last one of a long train," I said.

"Poor Nimita! I wonder how she has managed to go through this seventeen times?"

For the past two years, Mummy and Pappa's sister—

my *foi*—had been searching for a suitable husband for Nimita. Now Mummy was desperate. Even though Nimita had gone to SNDT Women's College and had a degree in home science, she couldn't see very well out of her gray-green eyes, and she was almost blind if the light was dim. There was a name for her eye condition, but I couldn't remember what it was called. What mattered most was that the doctor had told us that as time went by Nimita's vision could get worse, and eventually she could go blind. There was no cure for it. Not yet.

Today, the boy who was coming to meet Nimita had not finished college, but he owned his own business, a bangle shop in Bhuleshwar.

"If I were Nimita I would tell Pappa to stop the parade of potential grooms," I said.

"You would, but she is not you. I don't know what I'd do if I were in her place. It would be nice if I liked the first or the second person I met, and he liked me."

"For you," I said, snapping my fingers, "it'll be *chut mangani, putt shadi*—quick engagement, instant wedding."

"You think so?" Mohini said.

"Besides being smart, you're pretty and you have light skin. You have nothing to worry about."

"But you do?"

"Of course I do. All the boys want a pretty wife with a perfect set of teeth, who is about three inches shorter and three years younger than him and comes from a rich family. And has a whitish, or at least a wheatish, complexion."

"That's not true."

"Really? Find me one boy that doesn't want a perfect girl. Remember Rita living in the next building? Three boys rejected her because she has a slightly crooked smile."

"Jeeta, do you really believe that?"

"I do. And don't tell me you don't."

Mohini smiled. "You can charm any boy."

"I suppose I could, but he would have to be extra special not to care about my cinnamon-colored skin."

I wondered why the girl always had to be perfect. A boy could be dark and handsome, so why couldn't a girl be dark and beautiful?

"Let's catch a bus and go to the Chowpatty Beach before sunset," Mohini suggested.

I nodded absently. I was so wrapped up in my thoughts that I didn't hear what else she said. Before I realized what was happening, I'd tripped on a handcart and scraped my elbow. Blood oozed out of me.

"You need to wash your elbow and put some medicine on it. Let's go home," Mohini said.

"We've only been gone for ten minutes. If we go back, Mummy will be upset."

Mohini wrapped her arm around my waist. "I'm taking you home."

We returned to a full house. Mummy, Pappa, Nimita, Foi, and the three guests were in the living room.

Nimita was sitting up straight, as if she were afraid to breathe. It reminded me of the time when an inspector came to our school and I tried to look attentive and smart. Mummy, Pappa, and Foi were like the teachers trying to impress the inspector.

"What happened?" Mummy asked, but her eyes were saying, *you'd better have a deathly good excuse for showing up here.*

"Jeeta got hurt; I'll take care of her."

Mummy motioned with her hand for us to leave, and Mohini and I hurried through the room.

Silently, Mohini washed my elbow, put antibacterial cream on the wound, and bandaged it.

Then we waited in the bedroom for the boy and his family to leave.

They stayed for another hour. That was a good sign, I thought.

Not so.

The next day the boy's mother sent a message telling Mummy and Pappa they were interested in Mohini, not Nimita.

"But Nimita was the one who talked to him," I said to Mummy.

"Does it matter who talked?"

Nimita sat on a divan across from me, but I couldn't tell what she thought about all this. Nimita and Mohini were best friends and they talked all the time, *goos-poos, goos-poos*. Sure, they told me things that were safe to announce to the whole world, but nothing special, secret, or scandalous. "Did he seem nice? Did you like him?" I asked Nimita.

"What difference does it make?" Mummy said.

"If Nimita didn't like him, then—" I started to say.

"*Choop ker*, stay quiet! You're the one who dragged Mohini home."

"It was my idea to bring Jeeta home," Mohini said.

"Yes, but who banged into a handcart?"

"It wasn't planned," I said.

"I've never seen a girl as heavy-headed and long-tongued as you are," Mummy said.

Later, when Mummy was not around, I asked Nimita,

"Aren't you tired of seeing these boys? Don't you get mad?"

Nimita was sitting on a stool facing the dressing table. She didn't answer. Her lips were tightly pressed as she gave Mohini a glance in the mirror.

"Why don't you talk to Pappa? Tell him to find out more about the boy before you meet another flaky fellow."

"I can't."

"Why not? Doesn't it hurt to keep things all tightly knotted up inside of you? Doesn't it suffocate you?"

"You learn to live with a knot inside yourself, and after a while it doesn't bother you," she said, and then covered her face with her hands.

"Jeeta, that's enough," Mohini said as she walked over to us. She stood behind Nimita and began unbraiding her hair.

I ignored Mohini. "I waste my arguments on unimportant matters. I'm not asking you to be like me, but what if something really bothers you—"

Before I could finish, Mohini said, "You know what really bothers me? Your blabbering."

"Why can't I talk to Nimita? The two of you talk and laugh all day, but when I walk in you stop. When I'm around, you both whisper as if I'm going to steal your voices. It is always the two of you, Nimita and Mohini, Mohini and Nimita, as if you were a set of *tabla*, drums. Until last year you even walked to college and back together."

"You know Mummy doesn't want Nimita to go out alone," Mohini said.

"Yes, but I'm your sister, too. Why don't you include me?"

She didn't say anything. I stood there wanting to do something, anything, but all I could do was watch as Mohini moved a comb through Nimita's hair over and over again. "If you want, I'll braid your hair next," Mohini said to me.

A few days later when I came home from school, Mummy and Foi were sitting cross-legged on the kitchen floor drinking tea next to a big plastic bucket full of wheat.

"Where are Nimita and Mohini?" I asked Mummy.

"They went to Crawford Market."

"I wanted to go with them."

"What for?"

So I don't have to help clean the wheat, I thought.

"You need to go shopping as much as a monkey needs a ladder," Mummy said.

"Is there something you want?" Foi asked.

I shook my head. I wanted to shop with my sisters or a friend, not with Foi.

"Chiraj and Vivek have been out for two hours. Are they still in the courtyard?" Mummy asked.

"Yes."

"Still playing cricket?"

"What else?" My younger brothers, eleven-year-old Chiraj and nine-year-old Vivek, had each other and played cricket and marbles or ran around the courtyard with a dozen other boys all the time. As usual, I was left alone in the middle.

I wished I could invite my friends Yamini or Janki over sometimes, but because of Nimita's eye problem, Mummy had always been afraid of sending her to anyone's house and Nimita had never asked anyone to come to ours. Since she was the oldest, she set a pattern for all of us. None of us invited friends home.

"How are you doing in math?" Foi asked as she handed me her empty cup. I took Mummy's cup, too.

"So-so."

"I'm here all day. If you need help, let me know."

"Yes, get help now while Foi is here," Mummy said. "You can't afford to fail a subject and ruin your year."

"I'm not going to fail math or anything else," I said as I put the cups in the sink.

"Listen to the one with a rapid mouth."

"And smart brain," I said.

"And sparkling eyes," Foi said.

I gave Foi a smile as wide as a mango slice.

"Jeeta, you have such bright eyes and long lashes that even with your dark skin we'll find a good match for you," Foi added.

"Yes," I mumbled, biting my lower lip and turning away.

I liked Foi. Most of the time she was kind and sensible, but like other people I knew, she thought that light skin was the most important attribute for a girl, especially a girl of marrying age.

"Jeeta, is your mouth full of mung beans? Does it pain you to show a little more respect to your elders?" Mummy snapped.

"I'm sorry, Foi."

Gratitude or respect, I didn't feel an ounce of either. All I felt was fire—a rage in my heart that flamed through my eyes. I wanted to smash those cups against the window. I was tired of receiving such compliments. It was as if she had plucked a thousand feathers of happiness, and handed me only one.

I was convinced that Pappa had married Mummy because she had light, fawn-colored skin. But for me, it was as if God had used the special dark shade of the koyal bird. Lord Krishna's skin was rain-cloud dark and praised for its beauty in Sanskrit prayers, devotional songs, and popular movie tunes, but no one praised my skin—least of all, Mummy.

Two gray-blue pigeons landed outside on the windowsill. I'm not a pigeon, I told myself. I'm a dark, mysterious koyal bird, whose sweet songs inspire poets and writers. I had never seen a koyal in Mumbai, but I knew they were somewhere in the city, sitting on mango trees, singing in the morning.

When I came back to the kitchen after changing out of my school uniform, I heard Mummy say, "Pray for Nimita. If finding a husband for a daughter is as tough as swallowing metal pills, finding a husband for a daughter with a handicap is like *chewing* metal."

For the last several days, Mummy had been repeating that sentence over and over. The softness in her sigh had disappeared as quickly as the last prospective groom.

"Have faith and all will work out. It always does," Foi said.

"I worry about all my children; but for Nimita and Vivek . . ."

My youngest brother, Vivek, had the same eye condition as Nimita.

"Sure, Vivek has an eye problem," Foi said, "but it isn't as bad for him as it is for poor Nimita. In life, we womenfolk have more to lose and more to suffer than men."

"Isn't that the truth," Mummy replied, with a catch in her throat.

"Let me tell you about this new boy for Nimita," Foi said.

"Yes, yes, tell me all about him. What's his name? Who are his parents?" Mummy said, wiping the round, stainless steel *thali* with the edge of her yellow cotton sari and piling one side of it with wheat.

"His name is Girish Mehta, and he's an orphan."

"An orphan?" Mummy's mouth opened wide. Her hands clutched the edge of the *thali.*

Foi scrunched her eyebrows. A ridge rose instantly between them.

Mummy looked down.

"Listen to me before you say no, Purnima. Girish is from our caste and was raised in the Sheth Tejpal's orphanage right here in Mumbai. You know how careful they are to only take Modh Bania children in that orphanage."

Most of the time I found out about a new marriage prospect only after Nimita and Mohini did. Today, I was the first one to hear. I poured a glass of milk and dumped a spoonful of milk masala in it. I stirred as slowly and quietly as I could.

"I'm sure he is from our caste. But an orphan! Nimita won't have any family," Mummy said to Foi.

"We're not dead. And the fewer in-laws the better."

"Still . . ."

"Would you rather he had strings of brothers and sisters to be educated and married? You don't want Nimita to end up working like a donkey," Foi said, picking a tiny stone out of her wheat. Her blue sari had slipped from her chest, revealing a saggy breast through her thin blouse.

Foi never wore a bra. She always complained that the elastic band suffocated her. On the other hand, Mummy would never dream of going without one. Even after having so many children, Mummy still had what she called a "single body," and she was proud of it. She and our neighbor, Hema Auntie, categorized some people as "single-bodied" and other people as "double-bodied," as if those double-bodied people had stolen someone else's body and stuck it to their own. And then there were the people that they didn't know how to classify, and so they argued whether so-and-so had a single body, or a double body. I guess those people had a body and a half.

As soon as I had turned twelve Mummy handed me my first cotton bra. Every evening when she went to the temple, I would run to the bathroom and peel it off as fast as I could. At that time my chest was as flat as my forehead, and I wondered why she insisted that I wear a bra. But Mummy had reasons for her rules. I didn't always agree, but when I argued she got upset. It was best to leave the snake pit of her anger undisturbed.

"Without the family, how would we know what kind of a person Girish Mehta is?" Mummy asked.

"I've heard good things about him from many people at the orphanage. Just two weeks ago one of the younger students fell and broke his elbow. Girish took the boy to the doctor and stayed with him all afternoon."

That seemed to satisfy Mummy. "Where does he live?"

"At the orphanage. He does some work for them, and they give him a place to stay. The trustee said they will miss his singing when he leaves. He has a mountainous voice, deep and rich."

"If they decided to get married, where would they stay?"

"That's something we'd have to help them out with."

That evening I wanted to tell Nimita about Girish Mehta, but I never got a chance to be alone with her. Mummy must have told her after I went to bed that night, because in the morning she and Mohini went up to the terrace to dry saris. I followed them up and found them engrossed in talk. How I wished they'd make room for me to huddle up next to them so that our faces would touch and our breaths and whispers would mingle!

I sighed, turned, and came down the steps.

two

WHEN GIRISH MEHTA came to see Nimita, Mohini and I caught a glimpse of him as he entered the courtyard of our apartment building. Unlike the other suitors, he couldn't come with his mother and father, and he didn't bring an uncle, a friend, or even the director of the orphanage. He was a brave man.

I had always imagined that a groom would ride in on a white horse, wearing a long, silk *sherwani*, Jodhpuri pants, and a red turban. Girish would have looked good in those clothes riding a horse, I thought, but I doubted he knew how to ride.

Mummy, Pappa, Foi, and Fua, my uncle, were in the living room. After the last fiasco, Mummy asked us to stay in the bedroom. We sat on Chiraj's bed and played cards. Our L-shaped apartment made it possible for us to see what was going on in the living room from the bedroom window. It had always been our secret lookout.

We watched as Nimita brought tea and spicy, thin noodles on a tray from the kitchen. After Nimita served the tea I couldn't see her from the window, but I knew she was sitting right across from Girish.

"He's handsome," I said.

"Yeah, and that's not good," Mohini said, shaking her head.

"You think he'll refuse?"

"Probably."

But the next evening, Girish took Nimita out for two hours, and when they came back, he talked to Pappa and Mummy for a long time. Then we all met him. I noticed he had a pointy chin and large open eyes that made him look as though he were searching for something.

Before Girish left, Mummy brought out some brown sugar, and we all ate a bit of it. It meant that everything was decided. Pappa and Mummy were going to announce the engagement the next day, and have a small ceremony. To show Girish respect, Mummy began to call him Girishji, and so did we.

That night I lay awake thinking about marriage. It was

so different from all the Hindi movies we'd watched. In the movies, young people fell in love, sang songs, danced; and at the end of the story, no matter what, the hero and heroine got married. Where would the love be in Nimita's marriage? Maybe there was no love in everyday life. Maybe love only whispered in the hearts of poets, actors, and musicians.

And then I had a dreadful thought. What if Girishji never came to love Nimita? Would her soul stay as empty and lost as her eyes? Would she ever experience a flicker of his affection, or would her heart fumble like her hands did?

Now that they were engaged, Girishji took Nimita out every Sunday around five-thirty, and brought her home at eleven.

May first was set for the wedding date. Mommy and Foi made all the arrangements for the ceremony, the hall, and the reception. Pappa and Mummy paid for it all, as was the custom.

Nimita also needed saris and jewelry, so Mummy took her shopping every day. Mohini's exams were finished, so she went with them. I couldn't go because I still had to study for final exams. I was relieved, though. It was good to be out of Mummy's way when she was as tense as a stretched rubber band.

For the *garba*, a folk dance party two days before the wedding, I wore a satin skirt that stopped just above my ankles and a short blouse and a matching *odhani*, half sari. The skirt, the sleeves of the blouse, and the *odhani* were all embroidered with real silver threads. I draped the *odhani* over my right shoulder, pinning it to my blouse so it wouldn't slide off, and tucked the two free ends of it into my skirt. I wore a silver necklace, silver hoops, thin silver bangles, and silver anklets that Pappa had given me on my last birthday. I kept admiring the *mehndi* design that was painted on my hands. Mummy had organized a party the night before, and all the women of the family had had their hands painted with *mehndi* in intricate designs of flowers, fruits, vines, birds, the sun, and the moon.

With every turn, my skirt flared, my half-sari sparkled, and the tiny bells on my anklets sang. We danced in a big circle and clapped until we were dizzy and our hands were red and itchy. Then someone brought in a box of sticks, and the boys and girls and men and women paired up to do another folk dance called *dandia raas*.

A boy my age stood next to me. He wore a cream-colored *kurta-pajama* with a saffron-colored scarf tied around his waist. I didn't know him and wondered if he were from the orphanage. Before I could decide if I wanted to dance with him, someone began playing *dholak, dhamak, dhum, dhum, dhamak, dhum.*

I managed to give my partner a tiny smile before we started striking our sticks in a five-beat step. I twirled in and out of the circle around the boy. He kept the beat of *raas* like a real Gujju, a Gujarati, should. I was giddy with rhythm and motion, when Mummy pulled me out of the dance.

"What's the matter with you, Jeeta?"

"Nothing." I pretended not to understand what Mummy was upset about. But I knew she wasn't happy that I was dancing with a stranger.

"What makes you so bold? I don't want you dancing and smiling with a no-name person, for the world to watch."

"I am sure he has a name. He came over and stood next to me, Mummy. He seems nice."

"*Ja, ja,*" she said. "Nice, your tail. Do *dandia raas* with someone you know, or sit down." Mummy turned to Mohini, who'd just come over for a drink of water, and told her to stand right next to me to make sure I danced with one of our relatives.

My ex-partner stood waiting for me. I handed him my sticks and disappeared into the ladies' room, where two women sat nursing their infants. The infants' faces and bodies were completely covered with their mothers' saris, and only their tiny legs were sticking out. Since I didn't feel like smiling or talking to them, I sat in one of the chairs, partially covering my face with my *odhani*.

After a few minutes, Mohini came and asked, "Why are you sitting here? Come, dance."

"I don't want to."

"It's all for Nimita."

"Then she can dance."

"She'll miss you if you're not there. Let's make it happy for her. Please?" Mohini tugged at my hand.

I went out and did the *dandia raas* with Mummy's cousin, Kirti Auntie's son Meenal. He was fourteen and had no rhythm in his hands or legs. Several times he hit my fingers instead of my sticks, and twice he stepped on my bare toes, but at least Mummy was happy.

On the day of her wedding, Nimita wore a white silk sari with a red batik design. The gold thread embroidery was intricately woven into all six yards of the sari, and her silk blouse had matching embroidery on the sleeves. The twenty-two-karat gold jewelry that covered her neck, hands, and fingers was of the latest fashion, because Pappa worked as an accountant at the biggest jewelry shop in the Zaveri Bazaar.

"You look like one of the models for the jewelry-shop ads," Chiraj said to Nimita.

"Is this too much, Mummy?" Nimita asked, fingering her gold necklace.

"*Na-re-na*. What does Chiraj know about these things?"

"It'd be perfect to have the name of Pappa's shop on the back of Nimita's blouse. Just think how much business they'd get," Chiraj said.

"Why are you loitering around us women? Go get your turban tied," Mummy said.

He winked at Nimita and made her smile before he walked out of the room.

The wedding took place in a *mandap*, canopy, which represents the universe. When Girishji came to the hall, Mummy welcomed him and enscorted him to the *mandap*. Inside the *mandap*, Mummy and Pappa began the ceremony by invoking the blessings of Lord Ganesh. Then Nimita arrived escorted by Mummy's brother. She sat across from Girishji. Chiraj and I sat behind Girishji and Nimita, holding napkins and fans in our laps, ready to assist the couple during the long ceremony. I noticed that even in Nimita's hair, Mummy had stuck gold and silver clips.

When Nimita and Girishji put flower garlands around each other, the smell of roses filled the air. The priest recited a prayer seeking God's grace in the forthcoming marriage.

Pappa and Mummy gave Nimita's hand to Girishji, and the priest placed a sacred string around both of them, establishing a special link of mind, body, and soul. Now Mummy and Pappa were done with their part of the ceremony and left the *mandap*.

Since Girishji didn't have a sister, I had to perform the ceremony of tying Nimita's sari with Girishji's shawl. I made sure that the knot was tight and wouldn't come undone.

After Nimita and Girishji moved next to each other, the priest lit a holy fire that served as the divine witness of the marriage vows. Throughout all this, the priest chanted, and the photographer clicked away. Every time the priest called out "*Swaha*," Nimita and Girishji sprinkled rice or added ghee, clarified butter, to the fire. Luckily, in the noise and commotion, no one heard Chiraj when he asked me, "Does Nimita get to keep the gold she is wearing?"

"Those are her things now. She keeps it all," I whispered.

He stopped fanning Nimita and Girishji. "All that gold? How can that be?"

"Why? Are you afraid that by the time you get married there won't be anything left?"

"Why should I worry? I'm a boy."

"Napkin, who has a napkin?" someone shouted. Nimita had vermilion powder on her hands. I looked down and realized I had napkins on my lap. I quickly handed one to Nimita, but not before Foi had a chance to say, "Pay attention, children, we're here to get a daughter married, not to watch a movie."

Chiraj began to fan Girishji vigorously, and the flame roared.

I grabbed his hand. "What are you doing? Do you want to set Nimita's sari on fire?"

"I'm doing what Mummy asked me to do."

"Please . . . Will you two keep *shanti* now and do your arguing later?" Nimita said. After a few minutes Chiraj got up, saying he wanted a glass of water, and didn't come back. For the next hour and a half, I fanned Nimita and Girishji, handed them napkins often, and never once complained about the perspiration trickling down from my face to my neck and finally down my back. My head felt as though it were being baked by the flames of the fire.

Once in a while Mohini came near me but left quickly, dabbing her forehead with a lace handkerchief and complaining about the heat.

Now that Nimita was getting married, Mohini could

be seen and admired. Mummy had assigned her to greet the guests, so she had the perfect excuse to mingle with them and eat mango-saffron ice cream. I wished that during those three hours Mohini would transform from a single body to a double body!

In the evening there was the ceremony of *vidai*, or saying good-bye. The band rose and played some of the most melancholy tunes I'd ever heard. It sounded more like we were at someone's funeral to me. The brass *shehanai* player was particularly determined to play long, wailing sounds as Nimita and Girishji walked toward Pappa and Mummy to bow down and touch their feet. Mummy and Pappa blessed the couple, and then Mummy took Nimita in her arms, and they both cried. After that, the newlyweds bowed to Foi, Fua, and the other elders, and then began walking toward a marigold-and-rose-clad car.

Mohini held my hand, tears tumbling down her cheeks. Chiraj and Vivek stood on the other side of me, looking forlorn. Before getting into the car, Nimita turned around and rushed back to us. We, the five of us, held each other in a circle of ten arms.

Before the wedding, I had been afraid that I wouldn't be able to cry at the *vidai*, and wondered what I would do if my eyes stayed as dry as the Thar Desert. After all, Nimita was going to live right in Mumbai, and we were going to see her as often as we wanted. But I knew that as Nimita's sister, I must cry, so I'd made plans to dab spit on my cheeks. I didn't need to, though, because when Nimita got into the car, I could only see her through a veil of tears.

three

THE DAY AFTER the wedding, our neighbor Hema Auntie stopped by.

"It was a fabulous wedding. You didn't do anything less because of . . . you know what I mean. . . . He must have felt like a groom-king, despite the fact that . . . you know what I mean . . . he doesn't have any family."

"Yes, with God's wishes everything went fine," Mummy said, looking up at the picture of Lord Krishna playing a flute, a peacock feather adorning his dark, curly hair, and his eyes smiling at everyone. When I was four or five, I was afraid that if I didn't behave, his smile would vanish and he'd step out of the picture and scold me.

"Hema, come, come. Sit down," Foi said,

tucking in the loose end of her sari as she came out of the kitchen.

"*Kem cho*? How are you?" Hema Auntie said, looking a little startled. "I was telling Purnima that you didn't spare any expense for Nimita. You know what I mean. In these days of inflation, and when you have two other ones—"

Foi interrupted her, saying, "Hema, wouldn't you have done the same if you were in our place?"

"Yes, but Purnima still has two more daughters to worry about, and when her sons are so young, and one of them . . . You know what I mean."

"Everyone comes with their own destiny, and the giver has a thousand hands. Don't you worry, there is always a speck for an ant and a ton for an elephant," Foi said, sitting down.

Mohini brought tea out, and Hema Auntie took the hint and poured it into the saucer. She gulped it down without mentioning the subject again.

I wished Hema Auntie would stay in her own house and irritate her own family.

That evening, before Mummy went to Lord Krishna's temple, she asked Mohini and me to cook dinner. Now that Nimita was married, Mohini and I talked more. When

Mummy was away, the kitchen was our favorite place. No one could hear our *goos-poos*, private talks. Chiraj and Vivek were never around the kitchen. If I asked Chiraj to help with cleaning and cutting spinach or dicing potatoes, he always laughed and said, "I'm not a girl. I don't braid my hair and I don't dice potatoes." Mummy never asked him to help or expected him to serve a glass of water to a guest, so why would he listen to me?

As I stuffed round eggplants with a mixture of coriander leaves, fresh coconut, and spices, Mohini made dough.

I asked, "Do you know how much we spent on the wedding?"

"A lot."

"We must have. All the saris and jewelry we bought, and the hall rentals and food must have cost thousands of rupees."

"Yes."

I watched her divide up the dough into small balls. As she took a piece and began rolling it, I could see her brow arching and bunching up. I knew she was having a deep, troubling thought.

"Why did we have to do so much?" I asked.

"It's the custom."

"Does that mean we have to spend more than we can afford? Who cares about a stupid custom, anyway?" I said, dumping a spoonful of black mustard seeds into the hot oil.

"People care. Didn't you see how many relatives and friends came to admire all the things we gave Nimita?"

"What about you? They're talking about your marriage now. I heard Foi saying that a few people have approached with marriage offers for you."

"Have they?" Mohini said, with such urgency in her voice that I couldn't resist teasing her.

"You paraded enough at Nimita's wedding; you should be expecting it."

"Expecting what?"

"What do people do when they gather around? They talk and look for a boy or a girl for whoever is single. That's why Mummy and Foi had you all dressed up and prancing like a peacock in a monsoon. They wanted you to be seen."

She was quiet now, staring out the window.

"Don't you think?" I asked.

"Maybe." Suddenly, the smell of burning *rotli* filled the air, and Mohini whisked it off the stove.

I was glad that Mummy wasn't here. One thing she couldn't tolerate in us was not being able to make *rotli* right. "If a girl can roll out a thin, round *rotli* and cook it just right so that it puffs up like a balloon and has no black burn marks on it, then she knows how to cook," she would say to us.

"Are you ready to be married?"

"There is a part of me that is ready—ready to find someone who's brave, smart, and a survivor."

"You want your romantic hero to walk out of a book," I teased.

"I can dream."

"Yes, doesn't cost a rupee to dream."

"Only a *rotli* or two," she said as she took off another blackened *rotli* from the stove.

She spread ghee on two burned *rotli*, and we each ate one before Mummy got home.

Now that the wedding was over, we could go to the pool every day. The boys' and girls' pools were separate, but every morning Mohini, Chiraj, Vivek, and I walked two miles to the Mafatlal Bath together.

The first day after swimming, as we waited for Chiraj and Vivek, I saw three boys walking toward us. "*Ooi ma!*" I could hear my heart shout for the one walking on the right side, the side closest to me. He'd flung his towel like a scarf around his neck and was holding the ends. As he came closer to us I saw his eyes, as dark and dreamy as midnight. Maybe it was the dimples in his cheeks or the way his eyes brightened when he smiled that made me forget to breathe.

I caught his smile with my eyes and offered it right back.

Mohini caught me. "Why are you smiling at a stranger?"

"Just being polite."

"That's how it starts, you know," she scolded.

"That's how what starts?"

"*Lafra*, affairs, scandals."

"You have it all wrong. You're the pretty one and the smile is for you."

"I wish you could see your face right now."

"My face? What's wrong with it?" I said, wiping my cheeks.

"Everything is bright and beaming about it."

I could feel my ears turning red. "Don't you think he was something?" I asked.

"I guess so."

"You guess so? Tell me five men you know that are better looking than him."

"How about Ishan?" Last summer Hema Auntie's

brother, Ishan, had come to visit her. He had stayed for a month in the summer, but I had completely forgotten about him. I was surprised Mohini remembered him.

"He was good-looking, but too old."

"For you, maybe," Mohini said. Her eyes were all dreamy, as if Ishan were standing right in front of her.

"You mean he is the right age for you?"

"I didn't say that."

"You can have Ishan and I'll have this new boy."

"We're not going to have either one of them. Like Nimita, we'll have to choose from the ones Mummy picks out."

"Maybe, maybe not."

I wondered what other boys Mohini had liked in all these years. Did Nimita and she talk about Ishan? Had they met any other boys when they walked to college?

The first boy I liked was Kunal, who lived in our building. Even though I had known him all my life, right before my thirteenth birthday, something happened to me. From then on, when I saw him my heart started pounding as if I had run up the three flights of stairs to our apartment. Every afternoon I stood by the window when it was time for him to come home from school. I dreamed about what I would say to him if I accidentally met him on the stairs. This lasted for two years until Kunal moved to another city to attend college.

For the last couple of years there had been a few boys that I'd liked, but no one had stood out like Kunal, until today. On the way home I kept thinking, was the boy that smiled as handsome as I thought he was? Would he be there tomorrow? And if he was, should I smile at him first? If I saw him at the pool every day, then swimming was going to be my most favorite thing to do, for sure.

The next day, and the day after, and the day after, Mohini didn't scold me for smiling at the stranger.

On the weekends the pool had other activities and we didn't go swimming. Those days were as bleached out and colorless as the summer sky.

"Do you want to see a movie?" Mohini asked.

"No. The heat feels like a thousand ants are biting me," I complained. "I wish we could go swimming."

"Can't wait until Monday?"

I glared at Mohini. She put her finger on her lips and motioned toward Mummy, who was reading the matrimonial page of the *Janmabhoomi Pravasi*.

That afternoon Mummy's cousin Kirti Auntie visited us. After climbing up three flights of stairs, she was breathing wild and fast. Taking off her sandals and wiping the sweat beads on her forehead with a handkerchief, she huffed, "One down and two more to go."

"No, no, you made all three flights. Congratulations!" I said.

"Jeeta!" Mummy gave me a stern look as she folded the matrimonial pages, but I detected a tiny smile at the corner of her lips.

Kirti Auntie ignored me and asked Mummy, "Am I telling the truth or not?"

"You are. But the first daughter was the toughest, and the second is going to be the easiest, so don't worry," Mummy answered quickly. Then she let out her smile.

"Yes, yes. The second will be a snap."

I wondered how the third one was going to be. I guess Mummy didn't want to worry about my wedding until she absolutely had to, and for now, Kirti Auntie was in the mood to talk only about Nimita's wedding. For the next ten minutes, Kirti Auntie went on piling Mummy with praises. "Nimita was dazzling, her wedding sari and gold jewelry were exquisite, the garlands of roses were full of fragrance and the deepest shade of red, the smiles on the bride and groom's faces were those of the happiest couple; the work you'd put in was rewarded generously."

Puffed up with praise, Mummy's face glowed.

Kirti Auntie leaned over to Mummy and asked in a hushed tone, "Any good prospects for Mohini?"

"Yes, there are, but only a few are promising. One is the nephew of Mr. Maganlal Chaganlal."

"*The* Maganlal Chaganlal? The one who owns the tire business?"

"Yes, the very same one."

"I understand he doesn't have any family, so the factory will go to the nephew anyway."

"I don't think we're talking just because of the factory. . . ." Mummy said, faltering.

"No, no, of course not. I say, a hundred talks amount to one talk that matters, and that is, our daughters have to eat. Am I telling the truth or not? And we might as well find them rich men, especially for the pretty ones."

I knew by "pretty ones" Kirti Auntie meant Mohini as well as her own daughter, Jayshree.

For years there had been an unspoken rivalry between Mohini and Jayshree, who were only two months apart in age. They both had skin the color of sandalwood. Jayshree had a round face, with eyes that looked like they might roll off her face. Her nose was flat in the front, with tiny nostrils. A large black mole on her chin was striking, though, and transformed her ordinary face into a pretty one.

Mohini had an oval face, with curly lashes and a nose as straight as a candle's flame. She had no beauty mole, but her soft wispy hair always kissed her forehead.

Kirti Auntie had never considered me pretty. She used to refer to me as the one with *bhine-vaan*, a wet complexion. When I was little I didn't understand what it meant. One day, when I was about eight years old, I figured out that she meant dark-complexioned, like when a cloth is wet and it looks much darker than it does dry. So when she called me *bhine-vaan*, I said, "It's not as bad as *bhine-saan*, soggy sensibility, is it?"

After that day she stopped calling me *bhine-vaan*.

Kirti Auntie picked up the matrimonial pages and, fanning herself, asked, "Have you seen this boy?"

"No, we haven't, but we're meeting next Thursday."

"And who's the other one?"

"He's the son of the magistrate Kapadia, and he's only visiting for a month."

"From America?" Kirti Auntie's eyes widened and her lips parted as if she were going to gobble up a sweet, round *ladu* for dessert.

I wished Mummy wouldn't say any more. Her giving

all this information to the scheming Kirti Auntie made me uncomfortable.

I had good reason to worry, as it turned out. The next week, Mrs. Maganlal Chaganlal sent us a message that their nephew was engaged to be married to Jayshree, and so the Thursday meeting was canceled. Mummy was furious. "That Kirti didn't come to pay us a visit. She came to grab the nephew of Mr. Maganlal Chaganlal. Every time her mouth drips honey, I get stuck in it. I wonder what else is lurking inside her murky mind?"

Pappa laughed. "Now that she's taken her revenge, she might leave us alone."

I knew exactly what Pappa meant. Kirti Auntie was six months older than Mummy, and growing up, they attended the same school, ate in the same kitchen, walked to school together, and studied together. For years, they had played with each other and fought with each other.

When Pappa had gone to their house to meet his future bride, instead of one, there were two girls waiting for him. "Pick either one of them," Kirti Auntie's father had said. Well, Pappa picked Mummy, and ever since then Kirti Auntie has been furious with her. Like Mummy used to say, "*Kirti tikhu murchu che, khand ma boralu*; Kirti is a hot pepper dipped in sugar." Usually, Kirti Auntie hid her jealousy and anger well, but on certain occasions the sweetness melted away and the hotness stung.

"Don't throw away important matters in your laughter," Mummy said to Pappa. "Ever since Nimita got engaged I've been talking, listening, asking, and cajoling everyone about a good match for Mohini. Finally I find a good boy, and what happens? The crow takes the swan's sweet and you're as calm as frozen water."

"There's nothing to be done, Purnima. We haven't even seen the chap and now we won't have to take the trouble. I say it's a good thing Kirti went ahead."

Mommy threw her hands in the air. "I don't think you worry about getting your daughters married. That is all."

"I do. The future husband of Mohini is out there," he said, looking out the window. I looked out, too, but all I could see were four pigeons. "Eventually we will find him. No new one is going to be born for her."

"Old or new, it won't be this one, though, and what if Kirti goes after the magistrate's son, too?"

"Is she so greedy that she wants two husbands for Jayshree?"

"No, not for Jayshree. But maybe she wants him for her brother's daughter. She's only a year younger than Jayshree, you know. Oh, I wish a cobra would cross her path."

I smiled to myself, thinking it was very unlikely that a cobra would cross Kirti Auntie's path. There were no cobras in Mumbai except for the ones that the snake charmers carried in their baskets.

Pappa was tired after a long day of work, so I brought him tea. He took a sip and said, "Jeeta, I hope you find your own fellow to marry."

For this, Mummy was not ready. "Have your senses sunk? If she finds her own match, what would people say? What would we do?"

"She'd have a groom ready and we wouldn't have to do anything."

"What groom? What does she know about marriage and commitment? What about his caste? I don't want her marrying any useless fellow, a *hali-mavali* off the street." Then she turned to me. "Don't listen to your pappa. If you as much as go near a boy, I'll strip your skin off. We womenfolk have our reputations to protect. We're not brass pots that if dropped can be picked up and shined. We are earthen pots—once broken never mended."

I knew Mummy meant what she said. How could I forget the *garba* party at Nimita's wedding?

I was glad that Mummy didn't come to the pool with

us. If she found out that I was smiling at a stranger and thinking about him, she would scold me. But it would do no good. If I didn't have any control over my heart, how could Mummy?

four

NOW THAT NIMITA was married, Mummy expected me to help her and Mohini with the cooking. Sometimes I did, but most afternoons I played cards or *carrom* with Chiraj and Vivek. I never offered to make afternoon tea, and that didn't suit Mummy at all. "Playing with Chiraj and Vivek will never teach you a thing. Make good tea, learn to be a good cook; otherwise you'll ruin your pappa's name when you get married," she would say to me.

"How can I ruin Pappa's name? He's never in the kitchen and doesn't care if I'm in there or not. I'll ruin your name."

Mohini cringed.

"Did you hear her, Mohini? Every day Jeeta's tongue wags more and more, and I don't know what to do with her. She's so different from you and

Nimita." Looking at me, Mummy warned, "Don't behave like Pappa's spoiled potato. Learn to be polite and don't argue with your elders. If you can't do that—if you can't keep your long, unruly tongue in control—I'll pull it out."

Mummy felt that Pappa had spoiled me so much that there was nothing she could do to bring me back to her ways. It was true that Pappa and I had a special relationship. When I was little, I ran to Pappa if I was unhappy. He always lifted me up on his lap, listened to my complaints, stroked my hair, wiped my tears, kissed my cheeks, and brought a smile back to my face.

One of my earliest memories was from when I was four years old. Mummy had had a miscarriage late in her pregnancy, and I remember her lying on the bed in our bedroom. Many women came, and I heard some of them whisper as they left our house that whenever a family had a threesome, either three boys or three girls in a row, then something bad always happened.

I don't know who, but someone in a brown sari who smelled like a ripe, mushy banana, pointed at me and said, "This is the third one." She looked at me with such contempt that I ran to Mummy. Mummy was sitting up in bed, still surrounded by other women. I did not know any of those women by name, only by the smell of their saris: sour like three-day-old yogurt, sweet like talcum powder, nasty like used rags, starchy like overcooked rice.

After that I don't know what happened or what I did until that night, when Pappa made a bed for me on the divan in the living room.

He said, "Jeeta, come to Pappa." I couldn't even make it to his outstretched arms before I began crying. He put me on his lap, and I buried my face in his soft, muslin nightshirt and told him what had happened.

"I don't want to be the third one, I don't want to be the third one," I said between my sobs.

"I'm glad you're my third one. You are my Jeeta, my victory. You bring nothing but joy and love," he said. "Do you listen to the wandering street dogs that bark nonsense?"

I shook my head.

"Idle talk is like the barking of a dog. Don't listen to the talk and don't mind the talk."

That advice, for whatever reason, stuck with me. Meanwhile, Mummy gave me a lot of advice and made me aware of what people would say, but it all slipped off me, like water from a lotus leaf.

A couple of days later, Mohini had a cold and didn't come to the pool. After swimming, I took a quick shower and waited for Chiraj and Vivek, hoping they would do *thaga-thiya*, and take their time.

The three boys came out, and the one with the towel around his shoulders smiled, then stopped. "Your friend didn't come?"

Even though I'd pretended he smiled for Mohini, my heart sank. "My sister isn't well," I replied.

"I'm sorry. I hope you don't get sick."

"Hey, Neel, come on," one of his friend said, looking back.

"See you tomorrow," Neel said, and ran to catch up with his friends.

"Neel," I said to myself, and turned his name over in my head as if it were a piece of rock candy in my mouth. I liked the sound of it and its meaning. "Neel" meant blue, blue like Lord Shiva's neck, blue like a cloudless sky, blue like the Indian Ocean, and blue like a lotus, *neelkamal*.

On our way back from the pool, I thought about Neel. I wondered if he liked Mohini. He did ask about her, so he must like her. But when I told him she wasn't feeling well, he told me not to get sick. Does that mean he likes me? Mohini is so pretty! Everyone says so. Why would anyone like me over her? Yet he always looks at me and smiles. He stopped to talk to me. What does it mean? My head started spinning out thoughts that got all tangled up into a tight ball.

I wished I had a friend I could talk to.

Mohini, Nimita, and I planned to spend one Saturday together, just the three of us. We were going to a movie, to shop, and then out for dinner before taking Nimita home. The week before, Mohini and I had stood in a line for an hour to get tickets for a movie called *Soona Dil*, "Lonely Heart."

Mohini and I talked about it all week. We'd forgotten how it was to be with Nimita alone, without Girishji. Finally it was Saturday. Mohini and I waited for Nimita right outside the Opera House, under the gigantic billboard outside the theater. Girishji had promised to bring her straight there.

I'd seen the billboard from a distance earlier in the week. In the photo, the hero and the heroine were holding each other. The couple was draped in billowy white clothes against a pinkish-beige morning sky, as if they were floating down from their beautiful bungalow in the clouds. Her hands were around his waist and his hands were cupping her face. Their lips were slightly parted, ready to be united.

The flow of her dark hair and his dark head added vivid contrast to the rosy clouds. It was perfect.

Now, looking up from right below it, the picture had changed. The background was patchy and the faces were distorted and blurred. The parted lips of the couple had turned into seashells, and the heroine's hair into kelp.

The Opera House Theater was old and had been built for plays. The seats were arranged in a semicircle and gave a grand effect. Mummy and Pappa had seen their first movie together here, which made it special to all of us.

The theater stood on a busy corner, where traffic from Chowpatty Beach, Charni Road, Sardar Vallabhbhai Patel Road, and Prathna Samaj got tangled up. Across the street, the fancy, air-conditioned showroom of Jivan Raman Jewelers was busy. Dressed in a khaki uniform and a khaki cap, their doorman kept opening and closing the heavy glass door, constantly bowing to the customers coming and going.

The afternoon was hot, and I wanted a bottle of sweet-and-sour Limca. It would cool me before the movie started.

The ticket window closed, posting a sign that read, HOUSE FULL.

"Aren't you happy that we bought our tickets early?" Mohini asked.

"I'll be happier when Nimita gets here, then we can get out of this heat."

"She'll come. Have patience."

I dabbed my forehead with a handkerchief. A couple of black-market ticket sellers crept up to us. They flashed tickets in our faces and whispered, "Thirty extra, thirty rupees." I knew I would never pay thirty extra rupees for a ticket.

Two policemen stood fifty yards away from us. The police were supposed to stop the black marketers, but they ignored them. I wondered how much the black marketers paid the policemen to keep their eyes, ears, and mouths to themselves.

Mohini and I avoided looking at the black marketers and waited for Nimita, yet they kept hovering around us like pesky flies. Mohini pulled out the tickets and tapped them on her hand. Then other people began asking, "How much? How many?" Frustrated, Mohini slipped the tickets back into her purse.

I glanced at my watch. "Only five minutes before the show. Why isn't she here?"

"I don't know."

"If she's late, we'll have to walk into the theater in the dark."

"Maybe Girishji changed his plans."

"So? We haven't changed ours. Why does she have to do what he tells her to do? Being married doesn't mean you have to give up your freedom. Girishji doesn't have to give up his. Nimita has her own brains and she's not his slave. Why can't she decide what she wants to do and then do it?"

"But what if there was some emergency or . . ."

"That's different."

Fifteen more minutes passed. I was sure something dreadful had happened.

Then Nimita stepped out from a taxi.

"Where have you been? The movie is half over." I stopped when I saw Nimita's face. She had a look of a baby pigeon in a thunderstorm: confused and frightened.

I grabbed her hand. "What happened?"

"I . . . I just came to tell you that I can't watch the movie with you. But you two go and enjoy."

"Don't worry about us. Are you sick?" Mohini said, putting her arms around Nimita.

"No, I'm fine. I came because I knew you'd be waiting for me. I have to go back now, but both of you, please, go."

Mohini looked at me.

"We don't want to see a movie without you. Let's go home."

I flagged a taxi.

On the way, Nimita explained what had happened. Girishji was supposed to get off work at eleven, and then after an early lunch he planned to bring Nimita to the theater. Instead of coming home he called and told Nimita that his boss had asked him to do some extra work and that he wouldn't be home until two o'clock. When Nimita asked him if she could go to the movie by herself, he said, "What about my lunch?"

"I'll take out a *thali* and keep it covered," she said to him.

"I don't like eating cold food alone. You can see a movie next Saturday or the Saturday after that," he said, and hung up before she could say another word.

"I know how long we've waited to do this. I'm sorry," Nimita said.

"Why didn't you phone him back and explain to him?" I said.

"Because he wouldn't have understood."

"How can he not understand that we had tickets? For once, couldn't he serve himself? Would that have punctured his position?"

"It's all right. We'll go some other time," Mohini said. For the rest of the ride, Mohini held Nimita's hand and I stroked her back.

Nimita got out of the taxi at her apartment building and disappeared inside.

When we got home, Mohini said she had a headache. She slept for an hour, but her headache only got worse.

"Come, I'll rub your hair with oil," I said. From the shelf above the washbasin I took out a glass bottle filled with green oil. It was coconut oil infused with roses, *brahmi* leaves, *amla* fruits, and other plants. I sat on a wooden chair and Mohini sat on the floor. Slowly, I unbraided her hair, parted it, poured the oil directly on her head, and gently began to pat it. The fragrance was strong but soothing. Mohini's hair was as smooth as a marble pillar. I liked touching it. I massaged her scalp with my fingers, the way Mummy did when I had my headaches. It melted pain away.

"Mohini, I worry about Nimita," I said.

"Why?"

"Didn't you see her face? Girishji ruined our plans and she couldn't say a word to him. If I were her I'd be yelling like my braid was on fire."

"Nimita is not you. Besides, Girishji is not wicked or bad. Three times a week he brings her fresh jasmine *gajra* to put in her hair. He takes her out to eat, and remember on their first month's wedding anniversary he brought her that

French perfume? He just likes things his way, and when they don't go as he plans he gets frustrated."

"And he takes it out on other people."

"Nimita is not other people. She's his wife."

"So that makes it right? Makes it fair? What about us? Along with Nimita, our plans were ruined too."

"That's how he is. Maybe, slowly, Nimita can change him."

"How can she? Haven't you noticed how she puts her sandals on and stands by the door at five to eight, if he says he wants to leave at eight?" I knew that Girishji had left Nimita at home more than once because she wasn't ready fast enough, so now she got ready early.

"Like Mummy says, 'She's burned by hot milk, so she blows on her buttermilk,'" Mohini said.

"I wish she'd, she'd—"

"Shout and fight with him? I think patience and love are better cures, and Nimita has plenty of both. They'll be fine."

I picked up the comb, brushed out the tangles from Mohini's hair, and braided it.

"Are you better?" I asked, screwing the cap back on the oil bottle.

"Yes," she said, tilting her head back toward me.

"Sisters' hearts are strung together by gold thread. They never tarnish. I'm glad mine is strung on the same thread as Nimita's and yours."

I leaned over and kissed her forehead.

Every Sunday morning Pappa would go walking in the Hanging Gardens. Most of the time he would go alone, but sometimes if I was awake early enough, I would ask to go with him. On Sunday mornings the whole city had the feel of a majestic, undulating elephant. Most of the people were still at home, so I didn't have to stick out my elbows to get on and off the bus. The horns were silent and traffic moved smoothly, like a comb passing though untangled hair.

More than anything else, I loved being alone with Pappa—he and I, strolling in the beautiful Hanging Gardens.

That Saturday evening, after our missed date with Nimita, I wanted to talk to Pappa. It didn't happen. On Sunday morning I asked Pappa if I could go with him. He hesitated but then said yes. The red double-decker bus was almost empty, and we climbed up the winding stairs and sat in the front. From there I could watch the whole city as if I were watching a movie.

The conductor approached us with his leather pouch.

I paid him, took two tickets, and rolled them up. They reminded me of the cigarettes Pappa used to smoke. I unraveled them, smoothed them, and slid them into my skirt pocket.

We passed the Opera House Theater, then Chowpatty Beach, and finally began climbing Malabar Hill on Ridge Road. The Hanging Gardens was the last stop on Ridge Road, and the bus turned around to go back.

The steps leading to the terraced garden were freshly washed. *Chu-chee, chu-chee.* My sandals rubbed against the wet steps. The sun was still down, and the air was either too heavy or too tired to move. In Mumbai that was how summer heat always was: lazy, lazy, lazy. Only in the evening did the breeze come and nudge the heat away.

I'd been thinking about all that had happened yesterday. "Pappa," I said softly as we walked on the garden path, "is Nimita happy?"

"I think so. Yes," he said. His square jaw tensed up. It always did when he concentrated.

Pappa seem to have taken a long dip in his thoughts. I waited for him to surface.

As we walked quietly around the bend, I brushed my hand against the hedges. "*Ooi ma.*" They were as prickly as a bed of nails. Sometimes in the newspaper or magazines there were articles about a yogi or a holy man who walked on burning coals or slept on a bed of nails without being hurt. I was definitely not a yogi.

Even though the gardeners had been watering the area, the lawn and the shrubs wore brown patches in several places. We sat on a bench under a dusty hedge of oleander across from a giant cannonball tree. When the monsoon rain came, the cannonball trunk would be covered with pink-orange blossoms, perfuming the air.

"Has Nimita said anything to you?" Pappa asked.

"No."

He took my hand in his. Like his jaw, his hands were square and small. His fingers had square tips. A palm reader had said that Pappa's hands were those of a very practical man.

Slowly I began, "Yesterday . . ." and I told Pappa what had happened. He watched me intently. He didn't interrupt.

When I finished, he said, "Girishji is a loving, giving person. Nimita is the first person that has ever belonged to him, and he belongs to her. That probably scares him as much as it makes him happy."

"Why would that scare him?"

"That he might lose her. Remember when you were

little I used to give you coins to put in your piggy bank, but you didn't want to part with them? You used to fall asleep holding them."

"Yes. I remember. I was afraid that once I put them in the piggy bank, they'd be gone forever."

Suddenly, the koyal's call, *koo-hoo, koo-hoo,* filled the air. Pappa and I walked up to a tree where the song was coming from. We gazed up the tree, but we couldn't see her.

"I've never seen a koyal," I said.

"She teases with her voice, doesn't she?"

"Yes, 'Come and look for me,' she says."

"What else does she say?"

"I'm not telling; it's our secret."

"I'm glad you tell me some things. Without you I might not know half the things that go on in my own home."

"Mummy talks to you—"

"She does?" he said and smirked. "Yes, yes, she tells me all I don't need to know and a tiny bit of what I do need to know—"

"Pappa!"

"Don't you 'Pappa!' me. Come, let's go before sun heats up my head."

"Especially the bald spot in the back there," I teased.

Hand in hand, Pappa and I walked down the steps toward Kamla Nehru Park.

When I was young, I used to beg Pappa to take me to Kamla Nehru Park so I could climb the winding steps inside the Boot House and wave to him from the top. It had been a long time since I'd asked Pappa if we could go there.

From behind a bus a woman crossed the street toward us. I gasped. She had fans of peacock feathers peeking out from her back in a semicircle. It was as if all the peacocks of the world had chosen to display their shimmer and shine through her. Pappa looked at me and knew what I wanted. "How much?" he asked her.

"A hundred rupees."

It was too much. We turned away.

She followed Pappa. "What will you pay me?"

He didn't answer and kept on walking.

"Seventy-five rupees," she said as she held out three fans to me.

"Too much," Pappa said as he grabbed the bar to climb the bus.

"Sixty, for my first sale of the day. I'll have good luck all day."

"Fifty." Pappa reached in his pocket and pulled out his

wallet. She took the money and let me pick out a fan.

When we got home, Vivek kept turning the fan around and stroking the feathers."Is this your fan, Jeeta?"

"It's ours. We'll keep it here on the table in the living room and we'll all enjoy it."

"But is it yours? Do you get to take it with you when you get married?"

Ever since Nimita's wedding, Vivek talked about Mohini and me getting married and leaving home. He knew that it was inevitable. Bit by bit we were all going to peel away from his life, taking apart our family. He was the youngest and all he could do was watch it happen.

"I'm not getting married for a long time, and even when I do, I won't take the fan with me. I'll keep it right here for you," I said.

"Promise?"

"Promise."

five

IT WAS THE LAST WEEK of our swimming, and on Thursday, while we were waiting for Chiraj and Vivek, Mohini realized she had left her towel in the shower and went back to get it. I didn't see any need to drag behind like a tail, and waited in the lobby by myself. Neel's two friends passed by me, but he wasn't with them. I could taste my sour mood in my mouth. Finally, when I'd gathered enough courage to talk to him and had a perfect opportunity to do so, he wasn't here! Now there was only one day left.

I was absorbed in my thoughts when I heard someone saying, "Neel, we'll see you tomorrow."

I looked around and realized Neel was walking toward me. Say something, talk, I urged myself. But

what? It was hard to think while my heart raced away. I took a step forward. He stopped.

It took all my courage to say, "I thought you hadn't come today."

"I come every day."

"Do you live around here?"

"Yes, a five-minute walk."

"That's nice." I realized it was easy to talk to him once I had gotten past the first sentence. I glanced over my shoulder, hoping Mohini and the boys weren't back yet.

"Will you come to the pool when summer vacation is over?"

"I don't think so."

He was quiet. Maybe it wasn't the answer he expected or wanted to hear.

"Are you in college?" he finally asked.

"No, I still have one more year of school. What about you?"

Just then Mohini, Chiraj, and Vivek walked out. Neel must have seen something on my face, because he said, "I'll talk to you some other time."

Chiraj asked, "Who was that boy?"

"Just someone Jeeta knows," Mohini said.

"From where?"

"From somewhere, maybe she met him at Nimita's wedding."

"Jeeta, is he from the orphanage?"

Before I could answer, Mohini said, "Let's have coconut milk."

"I'm going to find the biggest coconut," Chiraj said. He grabbed Vivek's hand and they ran ahead of us.

"Thanks," I said to Mohini.

That afternoon, when Mummy, Mohini, and I went shopping, I ate *kulfi*. Mohini warned me against it, but the sun was burning me, and the thought of cold, vanilla-flavored *kulfi* melting on my tongue made me ignore her advice. It was creamy smooth and ice cold. A half an hour later my stomach rumbled, and it seemed like the food was climbing back up my throat. Mummy took me to Nimita's house, which was only five minutes from where we were. I lay down and rested for an hour.

Nimita begged Mummy, "Please, have a snack or at least a cup of tea. Otherwise you'll get a headache."

"Don't talk nonsense like a *pagel*. I will not have food at your house. I had a glass of water and that's enough for me. My mother never touched a drop of water at our house," she said proudly.

"Is it bad luck to eat at your own daughter's house?" I asked.

"No, it's not bad luck."

"Then why don't you?"

"Why do you eat my head with senseless questions?"

"I don't understand why you won't eat at Nimita's house," I said.

"Don't you see? Nimita belongs to Girishji now. I won't take from her."

"Will you take from Chiraj and Vivek after they get married?" Of course she would take from them. I knew that, but sometimes I pretended that I didn't. Mummy knew what I was doing and was furious.

"*Choop ker.* You're a *pagel.* Don't you see any difference between a son and a daughter? A son keeps his family's name and he belongs to his family forever. People pray to have sons. Who takes care of us while we are alive and cremates us when we die? Our sons do. Tomorrow all of you girls will take new names, but not my Chiraj and Vivek."

"We learned in science that both boys and girls get genes from their mother and father. They should be treated the same."

"This is not a science class," Mummy said, closing her eyes.

"In some parts of the world the women carry the family name; they're called matriarchal societies. In some places right here in India, it's like that. Do you suppose they aren't allowed to take from their sons' houses?"

"You lie there quietly. If it weren't for you we wouldn't be here."

I knew the tone of Mummy's voice too well to argue. I stopped talking and began thinking. What kind of logic was this? Didn't Mummy and Pappa give Nimita and Girishji this one-room home?

I scanned the room. It wasn't a huge, fancy place, but for a big city like Mumbai, this was as good as it got for a young couple, unless, of course, you were very rich. The kitchen was set up in the corner and consisted of a gas stove, a small refrigerator, and Formica cupboards to hold the dishes. Nimita had arranged the new stainless steel *thalis*, plates, small bowls, and pots on the bottom shelf, and glass bottles filled with various colored lentils and beans on the top shelf.

The sofa and two matching chairs were facing a television sitting snugly in a glass case with a cover. The bed and the steel-gray Godrej cabinet were in the short part of the L-shaped apartment. It gave privacy usually impossible to achieve in such a small place.

Because Nimita had vision problems, Mummy had taught her to organize things so she wouldn't have any trouble finding them. Nimita followed Mummy's advice, so her house always looked like it was ready for an inspection.

After a while I felt better, and I hung on to Mohini as we climbed down the dark stairs and walked out into the blinding glare of the sun. Then I felt sick all over again.

I couldn't go swimming the next day. I was so mad at myself for being stupid enough to eat something cold from a street vendor. When Mohini came home after swimming she said, "The teacher asked about you."

"Did you tell her I was sick?"

"Yes, I told her and also a couple of other nosy people who wanted to know where you were."

"Who asked about me?"

"No one special. Only the ones we see every day. I think someone else would have asked about you if I had let him."

"You mean Neel?"

She shrugged her shoulders. Why didn't you let Neel talk to you? I wanted to ask, but it was better if we didn't talk about him. If she pretended that Neel didn't exist, she couldn't ask me to stop smiling or talking to him.

I cursed myself for not talking to Neel earlier, for eating *kulfi* and missing the last day of swimming, for never asking him his last name. If I'm lucky I might see him next year, I thought. I felt like the sky burdened with the weight of dark clouds, mourning the loss of the sun.

On the first of June, three days before the beginning of school, Mummy asked, "What would you like to eat on your birthday besides *ladu*?"

Every summer I talked about my birthday until all of my family was tired of hearing about it. Last year Mohini had said, "If you mention your birthday one more time, I won't give you the present I've bought for you."

On my birthday I'd stuff myself with the *ladu* Mummy made, and couldn't settle down until Pappa came home. He always gave me gold or silver jewelry, and made me guess what it was until I got it right. Mummy thought it was a childish game, but Pappa and I had been playing it on my birthday ever since I could remember. I told Mummy, "Pappa and I will play it even when I'm forty and Pappa's an old man."

But this summer my thoughts were so stuck on Neel, I almost missed my own birthday.

"I'd like to have South Indian food," I told Mummy.

"Then that's what I'll make."

Mummy's Gujarati food, which we ate every day, was

delicious, but her South Indian food—crispy *dhosa*, steamed rice, and lentil cakes called *idli*, and spicy soup called *sambhar*—didn't taste like it should.

"Can we go out for dinner?"

"Out? What's wrong with my food?"

"There is a new restaurant called the Shree Café. It's on the way to the swimming pool and it smells so good when we walk by."

I didn't think Pappa was paying any attention to our conversation until he said, "How would you like to go to the fanciest place you've ever been?"

"Where?"

"Mummy and I will take you to the Taj."

"To the Taj?" Mummy said. "She isn't the only sister of seven brothers. If you spoil her, who would carry her burden?"

"It's my birthday." I said.

"So? Are you the first in the family to have a birthday? It's not like you have hunted a tiger, you know."

"If I'd hunted a tiger you'd have to bring me food in jail. It's illegal to hunt a tiger."

"*O mara bap!* You exhaust me like none of my children do," Mummy said, throwing her hands up in the air.

"Purnima, if you're already exhausted, I don't want you

to cook. Let's take Jeeta out to eat," Pappa said, and winked at me.

I thought about going to the Taj with Mummy and Pappa. I'd been in the hotel's lobby once, with its shiny marble floors and sparkling chandeliers, to buy pastries. It had made me nervous to walk across the floor, thinking I was going to ruin the place.

To go to the restaurant in the Taj would be special, but the prices on the menu would steal my appetite. And what would the three of us talk about? Mummy and I would probably just land in a jungle of arguments.

I asked Pappa if we could all go to the Shree Cafê for dinner instead, and he said yes.

When I found out Girishji couldn't come with us because he had an office party to go to, I was happy. I felt mean and guilty about being happy, but I couldn't help it.

The morning of my birthday, Mummy and I went to temple. The exquisitely carved sandalwood statue of baby Krishna was my favorite. His clothes were made out of turmeric-colored silk, and a peacock feather adorned his gold crown. I'd made a garland out of jaswanti flowers, and I handed it to the priest to put around Krishna's neck.

In the evening Foi and her husband, my *fua*, joined us

for dinner. For a birthday present, they gave me a gold-filled Parker pen set. The case was lined with red velvet. Both the pen and the case were so beautiful that I decided I'd forever keep them together. Nimita gave me wine-colored bracelets with sparkly white stones, and I slipped them on right away. They were from her and Girishji.

"Close your eyes," Mohini said.

She put something around my neck and fastened it in the back. When I looked in the mirror I saw the white-and-blue bead necklace that I'd admired a few months ago.

"It looks nice on you," Mohini said. Her voice trembled. I realized that this was the first time she and Nimita had not given me a gift together. I kissed her cheek.

"What do you think I bought you this year?" Pappa asked.

"A pair of earrings?"

"No."

"A necklace?"

"No."

"A pendant?"

"Yes, what shape?'

"Don't ask that; how should I know? A heart shape?"

"Yes. You got it right the first time."

"Oh, Pappa!" was all I could say when I opened the

package. The pendant was brushed gold with rays radiating from the center.

As soon as we walked into the Shree Cafê I could smell the sour tamarind-flavored lentil and vegetable *sambhar*. I ordered *idlis*. The fluffy, white *idlis* were served steaming hot with fresh coconut chutney and *sambhar*.

Fua ordered his food but we didn't know what he said, because he talked to the waiter in Kannada. Since Fua had grown up in Mysore, he was fluent in Kannada and whenever he got a chance to speak it, which wasn't very often, he did. I asked him what he asked for, and we were all shocked when he said he'd ordered a hundred-centimeter *dhosa*.

"That's almost as big as Vivek is!" Chiraj said. "I wonder how they make it."

I wanted to say, *Why are you so interested? You're a boy and you think you don't belong in the kitchen.* But Chiraj's dark brown eyes were wide with wonder and sparkled with admiration. Once he sees men cooking he might think differently, I thought.

"I want to see how they make it. Let's ask the waiter if we can watch the cook," I said.

"*Bess chani-mani*, sit and be quiet," Mummy said. "You don't help me in our kitchen and now you want to run to the restaurant's kitchen?"

"I'm not going to cook there." I smiled at Mummy, hoping she'd let us go to the kitchen.

"Jeeta, *Vatnu vateser shu kam kere che?* Why are you turning tiny talk into a twisty tale? Why are you being so stubborn?"

My smile collapsed.

Foi was sitting next to me. She patted my hand.

Mummy glanced at her and said, "Go, but be back in five minutes."

"Come," Foi said, getting up. "I'll take you and Chiraj to the kitchen."

Mummy lowered her eyes, and Chiraj and I went with Foi.

The Shree Cafê kitchen was long and narrow, and there were three people working in it. The head cook turned up the flame under the big iron skillet and stirred the creamy batter vigorously. He sprinkled some oil on the skillet and added a ladleful of the mixture to its center. Quickly, he spread the mixture in a circular motion until it covered the skillet's entire surface. He added a little more oil on the top and around the edges of the fresh *dhosa*, and let it cook.

It was hot in the kitchen, but I wanted to see how he flipped the *dhosa* to cook the other side. But the batter was spread so thin that he didn't need to. With a spatula he went around the edges and folded it over. Swiftly, he lifted the *dhosa* up with two spatulas, placing it on a plate, where it stayed like a rolled-up sheet of oversized paper.

"This *dhosa* is for all of us to share," Fua said. We each tore a piece of it for ourselves.

"I can never get my *dhosa* to come out so thin, crisp, and brown on the outside and so chewy and light on the inside," Mummy said.

Foi and I glanced at each other and covered the cook's secret with our smiles.

six

IT WAS MY LAST YEAR at the Majiraj School. It was an all-girls school, and most of my classmates had been with me since first grade, so I was surprised to see a new girl sitting three benches down from me. "Why would she switch schools for the last year?" I asked my friend Janki.

"I don't know. I wouldn't," she said.

Yamini turned around and said, "Her name is Sarina. Her father was appointed as a high court judge in Mumbai, so they had to move." Yamini was the gossip master of our school. It was nice for me, because she told me all she knew. I liked being on top of the news. And it didn't cost me a rupee.

The noise subsided as soon as our teacher, Mrs. Desai, walked in, wearing a starched light gray sari with a red border and a matching blouse. Every day she wore a thick gold necklace and diamond stud earrings, and between her two gold bangles she slipped on glass bangles that matched her sari, so today they were red and gray.

One by one Mrs. Desai assigned seats, and one by one my friends left me. Finally she said, "Jeeta Parekh in the third row with Sarina Shrimali."

I wasn't thrilled to sit with a new student. Often, they were *dodh dyha*, wise-and-a-half, which made other students look disorderly and ignorant. But Sarina's father was a high court judge and I didn't want to offend her. You never know when you might need the help of a high court judge, I thought.

I smiled as I sat down beside Sarina. There were just two to a bench, and I knew I must make her my friend quickly or else the year could be very long.

In between every class I talked with Sarina. She was tall with a copper-colored complexion. Her *mehndi*-conditioned hair was glossy with bronze highlights. It was as if she were born of fire, like Draupadi in the epic poem *Mahabharat*. Her arms and legs were long, and her eyes had a liquid quality that made her face soft like the rising sun.

She raised her hand in every class and answered every

question correctly. Her brilliance was overwhelming for an average student like me.

That afternoon at lunch recess she sat with Janki, Yamini, and me. Each of us had a *tiffin*, a three-tiered lunch box from home delivered to us by the *tiffinwallah*. Most of the students' stainless steel *tiffins* contained the same things: *dal*, rice, *rotli*, and vegetables. While we were taking out our food I noticed that Sarina came back empty-handed.

"Where's your lunch?" I asked.

"I don't know. It should've been here."

"I think the *tiffinwallah* have delivered for the day."

"Oh, no," Sarina said, looking around the lunchroom. Everyone was busy opening their boxes.

"Eat with me," I said. "I have more food than I can finish, and since it's the first day of school, Mummy has also packed a container of yogurt with sugar and pistachio nuts."

"Oh, no, I couldn't."

"Here," I said, serving her *rotli* and spicy peas and potatoes. "I never say no to food that's placed in front of me."

"Jeeta's telling the truth. She never does," Yamini piped in.

"It's because she has two sisters and two brothers," Janki said.

"She has only one sister at home now. Do you have any brothers or sisters?" Yamini asked Sarina.

"No. Only cousins."

"No wonder you're too shy to share my food," I said.

Sarina ate so daintily that it took her almost all of the recess to finish the food I'd given her. She can't eat this slowly at home, I thought. Either she's trying to impress us with her good manners or she doesn't like Mummy's cooking. The next day she did get her own *tiffin* and she still took bites as tiny as a fingertip. That was her habit. It seemed like a luxury an only child could afford to have!

After that first day, Sarina and I talked every chance we got. By the end of the first week I felt as though I had known her for at least a couple of past lives. I was intrigued by her travel stories and she was delighted by my family stories.

Sarina had traveled all over India. She'd taken a bath in the holy Ganga right where it touches the plains in Haridware. She'd ridden a camel in the Thar Desert and had seen lions in the Gir Forest. In a textbook, I'd seen a picture of the wall paintings at Ajanta. It was a picture of an *apsara,* a celestial dancer, in a beautiful pose, painted in the fifth century when the Gupta dynasty ruled India. I'd loved that picture. When Sarina told me that she'd seen cave after cave filled with paintings at Ajanta, I knew I had to see them too, someday. Her favorite memory was the sunrise and sunset on the Indian Ocean at Kanyakumari, on the tip of India's chin.

Sarina had traveled abroad, too. She'd been to places like Bali and America. I knew exactly where those places were on the map, but she'd actually been there. She'd seen the temples surrounded by lush gardens in Bali, and Balinese men and women wrapped in sarongs, shopping for their families. She'd traveled across the world to America and eaten pancakes and seen the Statue of Liberty.

I told her that I'd lived all my life in Mumbai except for two short trips. Once we went to Nathdwara for the first haircutting ceremonies for Chiraj and Vivek. All I remembered from that trip was people, people, and more people, and the towering, black statue of Lord Krishna called Shrinathji, and Chiraj and Vivek's bawling after they saw their completely shaven heads in the mirror for the first time.

On the other trip, we traveled by train to Sihor, Mummy's home town. I was only six at the time, but I could still picture the white marble temple of Lord Shiva on a hill, the saffron-colored flag and the small golden *kalash*, the dome on top of the temple, reflecting and radiating the colors of the setting sun.

Every day Yamini, Janki, Sarina, and I ate lunch together.

Even though Sarina became friends with Yamini, Janki, and a couple of other girls more quickly than anyone I'd known, I was her closest friend.

Soon after school opened, the monsoon season arrived and washed away the dirt and filth from everything—our windowsills, the road signs and signals, the buses, the leaves on the trees—and dumped it all on the streets, where it tried to flow into the backed-up rain gutters.

It was at the end of June, three weeks after school had started, when Sarina invited me to her house. I was excited and curious to meet her parents, but I was also nervous. What if her father, the judge, asked me a question I couldn't answer? If he was as smart as Sarina, then he'd be plenty smart for me. I didn't want to make a bad impression.

One Saturday, after our half day of school, I went home with Sarina. She lived on a side street off Marine Drive, by the ocean. Unlike the dark interior courtyard of our apartment building, her courtyard was open, with tall palm trees and potted flowers. A guard in a khaki uniform and matching cap sat on a wooden stool at the gate. He stood up and opened the gate for us.

The elevator man took us to the fifth floor. When a servant opened the door, the light coming from the big lobby jolted me. The blue of the Arabian Sea was deep, mysterious, and inviting. My heart pounded. I had no idea that Sarina lived in such a fine place. She never gave me any hint, but knowing that her father was on the high court, I should have guessed as much.

"Mummy, come and meet Jeeta," Sarina said, poking her head into the hallway.

When Sarina's mummy, dressed in a papaya-colored sari, came out, I got another shock. Her skin was the color of cloves, even darker than mine.

"Come in, come in," she said, putting her arm around me. "Sarina's told me so much about you. I've wanted to meet you since the first day of school."

I had no idea what to say to her, and stood there stupidly digging my toes into the lime green and coffee-colored silk rug.

"It's almost one-thirty. You two must be hungry. Go wash up and then we'll eat."

The sink was right by the dining table, and as I lathered my hands with soap, I tried to gather myself together. The judge was not home. That helped.

A servant brought the food out. Sarina's mummy, whom I called Mrs. Judge in my mind, ate with us and asked me about my family. There was something in her way of talking and listening that made me feel comfortable. She did not ask to be nosy or to put me down. I felt that she was interested in knowing me, her daughter's friend.

When I mentioned that Nimita was married, Mrs. Judge seemed surprised. I also told her about Nimita's eyes. Instead of saying how tragic it was to have a sister with such a problem, or congratulating my family for finding a match for her and getting her married, she wanted to know more.

"Nimita's vision is bad and it could get worse. She has a hereditary disease and there's no cure for it. My youngest brother, Vivek, has the same condition. My parents have tried everything, from seeing specialists to going to temples, but nothing has worked," I said, my voice shaking.

"Mummy is an ophthalmologist. Have they been to one?" Sarina asked.

"She's a real ophthalmologist?" I blurted without thinking. Mummy said I was too quick, and someday it would land me in icy water or a bucket of coal.

I turned to ice.

"Do you know any fake ophthalmologists?" Sarina asked, jabbing me with her elbow.

"Sarina!" Mrs. Judge said, and asked me, "Who's the specialist your sister and brother have seen?"

"I don't remember the name. I'll ask Mummy."

"Find out and let me know."

"I will."

I cursed myself for being stupid and rude. What could I say now? How? Where were my long tongue and sharp mind when I needed them the most?

"Jeeta, I didn't mean to upset you," Mrs. Judge said, patting my hand.

"Oh no, you didn't upset me at all. I'm feeling . . . I don't know . . . I'm . . . Thank you for caring so much."

"Sarina tells me your mummy makes the best mango pickles she's ever had."

"I think she does."

I was glad Mrs. Judge had changed the subject.

After lunch we went to Sarina's room. It was a beautiful room, painted in the lightest shade of blue, which reminded me of Neel. Besides her bed, there was a large ebony cupboard, a desk, and a wicker chair. Attached to Sarina's room was her own bathroom and a balcony.

I tried to picture a room that would have only my things: my bed, my books, my clothes, and my secrets. Mine alone. Our home was a one-bedroom apartment. All my life I'd shared a bedroom with Nimita, Mohini, Chiraj, Vivek, and Mummy. Pappa slept in the living room, and many times in the middle of the night, Mummy went there too, when she thought we were asleep.

Every night we put mattresses on the floor and spread white cotton sheets on top. There were two mattresses for Mummy, Mohini, and me; and Mohini and I rotated sleeping in the middle. Since Nimita couldn't see well at night, she got her own mattress and a nice corner to sleep in. Chiraj and Vivek slept on two single beds. After Nimita got married, Mummy slept in Nimita's corner and Mohini and I got our own mattresses, which made Mohini and me happy. No more sleeping on the crack!

"Let's go out on the balcony," Sarina said.

I followed.

From the balcony I could almost touch one of the palm trees. Looking up, I saw small coconuts hanging down like a bunch of green balloons. The sun sieved through the fingers of the palm fronds. Sarina's room didn't face the ocean, but from the left side of the balcony I could see a sliver of it. It didn't matter. The breeze fluttered the scent of the ocean to us.

"Only yesterday, after the first rain of the monsoon, did we turn off the air-conditioning. It feels good to open up all the windows and doors and smell the earth, doesn't it?"

"We don't have AC," I said, holding the horizon with my eyes.

She put her hand on my shoulder. "In Mumbai you really don't need it anyway. It never gets that hot here. For a few years, we were in New Delhi and it got so hot there that I wished I were a water buffalo sitting in a muddy pond. If you ever live there, make sure you have one."

"A pond or a buffalo?"

She laughed. "No. I meant an air conditioner."

"Oh!" I said. "We're not rich. We only have one apartment in Mumbai. I could never imagine having a place in two cities. You know, I've never lived anywhere but Mumbai and I don't think I ever will."

"Why not? We're not rich either. We get this apartment to live in because Pappa is a judge. In Delhi we also had a nice place to live, but we didn't own that place either. In fact, Pappa jokes that someday before he retires we'll have to find a place of our own to live in. Mummy and Pappa say that they never imagined they'd live in such a fancy place. So you see, you never know. You might live in Delhi or somewhere else."

"You mean, get married to someone who's not from Mumbai?"

"Get married! I wasn't thinking about that. What if you go somewhere to study or work?"

I stared at her.

The thought of my going far away to study or work had never occurred to me. In my house the conversations were always about getting someone married. First it was Nimita, now it was Mohini, and I knew that as soon as Mohini was married, Mummy would start thinking about me.

"Why didn't you tell me that your mummy was a doctor?" I asked.

"Was I supposed to? You never asked me what she did."

"I never thought about it. I always thought of her as, as . . ."

"Mrs. Judge?" Sarina laughed. "One time you did call her that."

I could feel the blood rushing to my ears.

"I'm sorry. It's just that when I found out your pappa was a judge, it was easy to think of her as Mrs. Judge."

"Now you can call her Mrs. Doctor, and Pappa Mr. Judge."

"Or I could call them Mrs. and Mr. Doctor."

We sat on Sarina's bed and talked for a long time. Usually I talked a lot, but today I listened. "Do you want to see pictures of my trip to America?" she asked, pulling a paisley-patterned album out of her bookshelf.

"You went all the way to America and stayed with a family for six weeks? I can't imagine doing that. Are they your relatives?" I said, resting the album on my lap.

"Oh, no."

"Did you know them well?"

"Not at all. I met my host family for the first time when I went there. Here are my two sisters."

"You don't have sisters."

"Not like you have Nimita and Mohini," she said. "When you go and live with a host family, you become part of their family. Since last summer I've had two sisters."

Sarina's sisters had golden hair and blue eyes, like fairies. Everything in the pictures of America looked so different. The house had no front courtyard or gate, but the ground was covered by a carpet of grass that led to the front door.

When I asked Sarina if *neem* or mango trees grew there she said, "Not in the Midwest, because in winter, it gets very cold and snowy there. They wouldn't survive." She showed me pictures of beautiful trees called linden, ash, and birch. I could not imagine such a lush place getting cold and snowy. She pointed out a bird, the color of our double-decker bus, called a cardinal; an ocean-colored bird called a blue jay; and an orange-breasted robin. As we flipped the pages of the album, part of me felt as though I'd been there too.

When we finished looking at her pictures, there were so many questions I wanted to ask, but I didn't. I'd made a fool enough of myself for one afternoon.

"Let me call and see if my cousin is home," Sarina said. "Maybe he can come over for a while."

While she dialed I looked through her album one more time. All those places, filled with flowers and sunshine, looked like they belonged only in paintings.

"We just missed him. Isn't that terrible?" she said, hanging up the phone.

That day I had met Sarina's mummy, and that was enough. I had no idea what her cousin was like, but I was relieved we had missed him.

When I got home, I wanted to tell Mummy all about Sarina, but I couldn't. It was a big day at the temple and Mummy wanted to be there. While Mohini and I made dinner that evening, I talked about my afternoon with Sarina.

"I wish we had a cook like hers, then we wouldn't have to work in the kitchen," Mohini said.

"Cooking isn't so bad. I wish we could travel like her."

"What's wrong with Mumbai?"

"Oh, Mohini, you should've seen the pictures of her other family in America. It looked so different from anything we could ever imagine. A bird called a cardinal was the color of red oleander, and the grass looked like someone had spread a green sari on the ground. And her two sisters had hair the color of a lion's mane."

"Her sisters? I wouldn't want to call some strange girls my sisters, would you? That's not her real family. Are they from her caste or Gujarati or even Indian? How could she make them her sisters?"

"I don't know," I mumbled.

That night I couldn't fall asleep. I kept turning from my left side to my right side and then back to my left. I turned over on my stomach until I had a stomachache. Then I flipped on my back, staring at the whirling dark blades of the fan until I was going round and round with it.

I closed my eyes and thought about Sarina and Mrs. Judge. I liked both of them a lot. They lived so differently than we did, not just with the big apartment and all that, but in their thinking and in their actions. I searched my memory, but failed to remember Mummy ever taking time to talk to one of my friends. How could a friend of mine have anything important to say to her? Mrs. Judge wasn't just friendly. I saw kindness in her eyes and concern in her voice when she heard about Nimita. I knew that as soon as she heard of any cure for Nimita and Vivek's eye condition she would tell me.

And Sarina! She believed in me. She thought I could go far away to study or work or travel. I liked the way she made me feel. It was as if I had powers—powers to do what I wanted to do, be what I wanted to be.

seven

BY JULY, the monsoon had dunked the city soggy. Just outside our courtyard I would wait for the school bus to pick me up, usually dressed in a raincoat and plastic gum boots that came halfway up my calves. Some days the sky turned so dark, it was hard to tell what time it was.

When it rained thirty inches in three days, our classes were canceled. In the past I would have played *carrom* with Chiraj and Vivek, but now I studied more.

I'd never thought studying was important, because I didn't know what good it did to read, count, and stuff my head with words, numbers, and formulas, when all I was going to do was get married, keep my in-laws happy, and worry about my daughter talking to a stranger.

Now that I was friends with Sarina, school seemed different. It was a place where I could excel, and if I did, there would be other places I could go—places I'd never thought of before.

Sarina raised her hand in all our classes, from science to Sanskrit. It encouraged me to participate in class, and the more I did, the easier it got.

At home, the first thing I did was finish my homework before watching TV or wasting time arguing with Chiraj. Mummy thought that I was hiding behind my books to avoid housework. When I showed her my test results she said, "I hope you didn't cheat, did you?"

Her words were like a hot coal pressed against my heart. Even after they were gone I could feel the pain.

When I was seven years old, I'd had typhoid fever and missed so much school that I had to repeat the third grade. From then on, I had been one of the oldest students in my class. Every year, the new teacher looked at my past record and thought that I was too lazy or too stupid to pass the third grade. No one cared to know the real reason. Mummy knew it, yet she still said things that hurt me.

"No. Sarina helped me and I worked hard," I said with forced calmness.

"All these years you must not have paid any attention

in class. Look what you can do if you use your brain."

"I know." I walked away. At times like this I wished I had my own room, even a closet.

When Pappa saw my report card, he was very impressed. "We must start thinking about colleges for you," he said.

"Yes," I said, laying my head on his shoulder.

When the monsoon finally began to wind down, we could sit out in the school courtyard at recess. I loved walking outside after a light rain when the air carried the earth's water-soaked smell. One day at recess while Janki was on monitor duty, Yamini, Sarina, and I sat on a stone bench. Yamini sat in the middle to show us pictures from her trip to Kerala.

"Who is this?" Sarina gasped, taking a picture from Yamini's hand.

"That's me," Yamini said, pointing.

"I mean the guy. Who is he?" Sarina's voice was high and she sounded eager, impatient.

"That's Kiran."

"Your brother, Kiran?" I said. Kiran was two years older than Yamini. When we were younger he used to come to pick up Yamini. At that time his arms and legs looked like they needed to be shortened to fit his body. I hadn't seen him in three years.

"Yes."

"He looks like—like he's modeling the spring collection of Rohit Bal," Sarina said.

Yamini laughed. "My brother, a model?"

"He's such a dream," Sarina said.

I'd never heard her talk like that about a boy before. It surprised me and made me curious. Had Kiran grown handsome in three years? I leaned over to look at the picture.

"I don't think anyone has ever told Kiran that," Yamini said. "He is too tall, too thin, and has too long a face to be a dream."

Sarina was staring at the picture.

"I'll tell my brother that my friend Sarina thinks he's a nightmare," Yamini teased.

"You'd better not say that."

"Sorry. I'll tell him you think he is a *drrrrream*."

"Don't."

"You'd better come to my house, Sarina, and tell him whatever you want to tell him yourself," Yamini said.

"Maybe I will."

"Why are you so quiet?" Yamini asked me.

"Maybe Jeeta doesn't want me to see your brother. Maybe she likes him."

Even though I'd not seen Neel in weeks, his smiling, dimpled face and dark eyes were as real to me as if I'd seen him yesterday. "You can have Kiran," I said.

"Jeeta is going to wait until she meets her dream boy from the matrimonial section," Yamini said.

" 'Gujarati parents invite correspondence from a beautiful, slim girl for their handsome, five-foot-eleven, professional son. Please reply with a picture, bio-data, and horoscope.' " Sarina rattled off a matrimonial ad.

Yamini asked, "How about 'girl with strong east-west family values'?"

"Yeah, let's throw that in there, too."

"They always want a fair girl, so I won't qualify. Besides, I don't need matrimonial ads. I'll take care of myself," I said, and got up.

"She's still thinking of that fellow she told us about—the one she met at the swimming pool last summer," Yamini said.

I couldn't stop a smile.

"I don't think Jeeta told us his name. He does have a name, doesn't he?" Sarina asked.

I hesitated a moment before saying, "Neel." It was the first time I had said his name out loud.

"That's a nice name," Yamini said.

Sarina was quiet, as if I'd said something that made her think of something or someone. "Neel who?" she asked.

"Neel. Just Neel. I don't know his last name."

"Where does he go to school? Or is he in college?" Yamini asked.

I remembered the time Neel asked me if I was in college. "I think he's in college, but I don't know which one."

"You liked this guy from the first day of summer, saw him every day at the pool, and you still don't know his name beyond Neel? You don't know which college he goes to?" Yamini said, shaking her head.

"Well, I'm sorry. I should have asked him for his biodata so I could pass on all the information to my nosy friends."

Later that day, when it was just the two of us, Sarina asked me, "Did you meet Neel at the Mafatlal Bath this summer?"

"Yes."

"What does he look like? Did you talk to him at all?"

I told her about his thick brown hair and dimpled smile, and the two conversations I had with him. I didn't tell her about his midnight-dark eyes. I wanted to keep that for myself.

After listening to me, Sarina asked, "Have you seen him since the summer?"

"Oh, no, I haven't."

"Why?"

"Because I haven't gone to the pool since then. Anyway, if Mummy found out about it she would—she doesn't want me to talk to boys.

Her eyes narrowed. "*Gappa!* You're lying!"

"No *gappa*. I'm telling you the truth. Mummy absolutely forbids us to talk to boys."

I didn't know if Sarina believed me or not, but she didn't ask me any more questions about Neel.

Two days later Yamini invited Sarina and me to her house. I wanted to go, but I knew Mummy wouldn't allow it, so I told Yamini I had to visit Foi and Fua.

The day after Sarina went to Yamini's house I asked, "Sarina, did you meet your dream?"

"Yamini lied. She promised me that I'd see Kiran, but he wasn't home."

"I didn't know he had a biology lab to make up. He came home late," Yamini protested.

"If I'm supposed to meet him, someday I will."

"What do you mean?" I asked.

"If Kiran and my karmas are connected, we'll meet. Otherwise, no matter how hard we try, it won't happen."

I thought about this and wondered if my karma was connected with Neel's—or with any other boy's, for that matter.

By October the rain was gone and the skies cleared. The days were hot but the nights were as soft as moon's kisses. Every year I waited to devour the months from October to February.

One day when I came from school, Mummy was beaming like the universe had opened up a secret to her. "Nimita is pregnant," she whispered.

"When did she find out?"

"Just today."

"Why are you whispering? No one is around."

"We don't want to announce it to the whole world, do we?"

"Well, in a few months it will announce itself, won't it?" I said, washing my hands.

"Until then we have to be careful."

"Yes, these days our walls and windows gossip."

"I tell you—"

"I know, my tongue wags too much," I said as I broke off a piece of *chiki*, a peanut and brown-sugar candy.

Now that Nimita was pregnant, Mommy invited her and Girishji to spend every Sunday with us. They arrived at noon and didn't leave until eight. Mummy and Mohini would spend all morning cooking. Because twelfth grade is the most important year of school, I didn't have to help with cooking, but I had to help serve the food.

For Sunday lunch Mummy would cook two or three curried or stuffed vegetables, curried lentil soup called dal, fancy basmati rice with cashews and raisins, and a salad of shredded carrots, cabbage, and bell peppers with a hint of lemon and ginger. She made a dessert called *shrikhand* by draining yogurt in a colander lined with muslin and adding sugar, saffron, and cardamom to it. It was Girishji's favorite. After having the same dessert for two Sundays in a row, I didn't care to eat another spoonful of it. Sometimes Mummy stuffed spicy peas and a coriander mixture into mashed potato pockets and then deep-fried them. It took her and Mohini the entire morning to make this special lunch. I felt a little guilty for not chopping cabbage, shelling peas, mashing potatoes, and making chutney, but mostly I was glad.

Mummy made hot *rotli* and told Mohini to spread a generous amount of ghee on them and serve them to Girishji as fast as he could stuff them in his mouth. I don't think Girishji's own mother would have fed him so well.

At lunch, Mummy served Girishji and Pappa first. Occasionally, she asked Chiraj and Vivek to join them, but never Mohini or me. Mummy treated Girishji almost like a lord, serving him food on the shiniest, newest *thali*. Because Nimita was expected to be embarrassed to serve Girishji in front of Pappa, Mohini and I had to hover around him like flies around food.

I hated Girishji for ruining every Sunday for Mohini and me. I wished he had a large family of three sisters and four brothers. Then he and Nimita could visit all of them, and our turn would come only once every two months or so. I loved Nimita, but she was married now and always came with Girishji. Just because she was pregnant didn't mean she had to spend every Sunday here, did it? And if she did, couldn't she leave him behind? Just once, couldn't she and Girishji sleep late and not show up?

On Sundays we didn't eat our lunch until two in the afternoon. And then we had to be quiet because Pappa rested on one bed and Girishji on the other. Chiraj and Vivek played cards on the apartment building's stairwell landing between the second and third floors. Our servant, Naran, cleaned the dishes in the kitchen, and so the only place left for us was the living room. Mummy never rested during the day. As she sat and embroidered a sari border, Nimita took a nap on the divan, and Mohini read a novel by Munshi, Meghani, or Dhumketu. Unlike Mohini, I could never read a book ten times over, even if it was about kings, queens, valiant warriors, and beautiful temple dancers.

So in the afternoon I would study with half a mind on my homework and half a mind on summer and the swimming pool and Neel. I wished I'd met Sarina last year. Then I would have talked to her about Neel and might have been bold enough to get to know him better.

After receiving my report card for the first quarter and watching me study hard, Mummy became curious about Sarina. She asked what Sarina's mummy and pappa did, if she had any brothers or sisters, and where they lived before moving to Mumbai.

I'd already told her what Sarina's parents did, that she was an only child, and that they'd moved from New Delhi. Maybe she hadn't been listening.

One Friday, after I got a hundred percent on my math

test, Mummy kept looking at my test paper over and over again. "All I can say is, when your luck arrives, it drops right through the roof and lands in your lap."

I looked at my lap. "I don't see anything sitting on my lap."

"Sarina is your luck. She's turned your lazy brain inside out, hasn't she? Ask her to have lunch with us on Sunday."

"Lunch? Sarina?"

"Yes. I want to meet her."

Once when I was in seventh grade I had asked Mummy if Janki and Yamini could come over. Mummy said, "There are five of you. Isn't that enough? Why do you need two more?"

Sarina had worked her magic on Mummy without even trying. I wondered if it was a bad idea to have Sarina eat lunch with us. What would she think of Mummy serving Girishji and Pappa first?

"I'll ask her," I said, praying Sarina would decline the invitation.

No one heard my prayers.

On Sunday, Sarina came to our house at eleven-thirty sharp. I ran from the bedroom to open the door, but when I got there Mummy had already opened it. "Come in, come in," Mummy said, her voice and the tinkling of her gold bangles singing out in unison. She gave Sarina a smile as wide as the open door.

After introducing Sarina to my family I wished I hadn't invited her. Our apartment was so small that there was no place to go. We had no galleries to sit in and watch the ocean and feel the breeze. Our bedroom windows with their iron bars looked more like jail windows, and there was absolutely no view except of the pigeons and their mess on the windowsills. The two of us sat on Vivek's bed.

While Sarina and I talked, everyone else stayed out of the bedroom, and an hour later Mummy came and asked us if we were ready to eat.

"You two and Mohini can eat with Pappa and Girishji."

I started to say something, but stopped, catching my surprise before it escaped through my mouth. That day Mummy served us, and I felt like a stranger in my own home.

After lunch we all sat together in the living room. With so many people around, I thought that Sarina would feel uncomfortable, but she didn't seem to be. At first she was a little shy, but when Mohini asked her about her trip to America she started talking. My family listened to Sarina. Pappa and Girishji didn't yawn, Mummy focused her eyes on Sarina, and Chiraj and Vivek sat still.

Like the Binaca toothpaste advertised on the radio, this was my new, improved family, leaving nothing but a clean, sparkling taste behind, I thought.

After Sarina's visit Mummy let me go to Sarina's house as often as I wanted. Sarina came over too, but I preferred going there. Mummy definitely treated Sarina differently than she treated my other friends.

When Yamini or Janki stopped by to borrow a book or notes, Mummy would keep on with her work. They were not important to her. Once, I came back from Yamini's house and told Mummy about Yamini's two older brothers, and that was it. I was never allowed to go to her house again. Yamini and Janki invited me a few times after that, but I made excuses. Then they started making plans without me.

Then there were boys. I thought it was really silly of Mummy to keep me away from them. Did she believe it would make me stop thinking about them? Did Mummy think that just because she sent me to an all-girls school, we never talked about boys?

"I'm glad Mummy lets you go to Sarina's house," Mohini said to me one day while we were sitting in the kitchen. She was slicing guava.

"I'm afraid, though," I said, sprinkling salt and black pepper on the pink flesh of the guava.

"Why?"

"You know Mummy. One day a worm of doubt will wiggle in her head and then she won't let me go."

"I don't think so. She likes Sarina a lot."

"Yes, but even before Mummy had met Sarina, she let me go to her house."

"I wonder why," she said, picking up a slice.

"Because Sarina's smart?"

"Sweet."

"Sarina, Mummy, or the guava?" I asked. Mohini couldn't laugh. Her mouth was full of guava. I ate a slice, and its sweet, tart flavor, boosted by salt and pepper, soaked my tongue.

"It's not only that Sarina's smart, her parents are educated and influential too," Mohini said.

"Don't forget that she doesn't have any brothers. Mummy doesn't have to worry about my seeing any boys. Don't you think if Sarina had an older brother Mummy wouldn't like her as much?"

"Mummy would like Sarina the same but she probably wouldn't allow you to go to her house."

"Probably wouldn't? There's no 'probably' about it. She definitely wouldn't allow me." Even though I was eating sweet guava my words tasted bitter.

"I know that sometimes you think Mummy lives in the last century, but you have to put yourself in her place. It took her such a long time to find a match for Nimita, and now she has to worry about getting us married. People like Kirti Auntie are of no help and make Mummy miserable. Don't you see? All Mummy wants is for all of us to be happy."

"Then why doesn't she let us do what we want, like Pappa? Wouldn't that make us happy?"

"Pappa is a man. He doesn't understand how it is to be a woman. Remember that Pappa didn't find Girishji for Nimita. Mummy and Foi did. All day long, every day, who's with us? Mummy, not Pappa. They both love us. Pappa works hard for us, but Mummy molds us."

"Molds us for what?"

"Molds us so we can live in this society," she said, picking up another slice of guava.

"I don't want to be molded. Besides, we have brains up there, not *rotli* dough."

"You remind me of Manjari."

Manjari was a teenage character in Mohini's favorite novel, *Gujaratno Nath.* Manjari was arrogant about her knowledge and proud of her intelligence.

"At least Manjari thought for herself. What good does

it do for you to read all those books and do what Mummy wants you to do?"

"Jeeta! We're not characters from a book. In the summer you smiled at that boy every single day. If I hadn't been there, you would've talked to him and—"

"What's wrong with that?"

"It could lead to other things."

"Sarina says that in America—"

"This is Bharat, India. That's what I've been trying to tell you."

"Sarina has friends that are boys."

"It's different for Sarina. She's an only child. She doesn't have Nimita and Vivek to worry about. Her parents know influential people like themselves."

"You mean she has more freedom because of that?" A guava seed had found a home between my teeth, and my tongue kept visiting it.

"Yes."

"I hope Mummy will always like Sarina."

"She will. You shouldn't have any reason to worry about her stopping you from going to Sarina's house."

While I was brushing my teeth to dislodge the seed, I thought about what Mohini had said to me. She seemed to understand Mummy much better than I did. It had always been that way. I wondered who would explain Mummy to me after Mohini got married.

For the past few days Mummy had been excited. She'd found out about one Mr. Kapadia, who was coming from America to celebrate Diwali and get married. Pappa was right. Mohini's future husband was definitely out there, and Mummy was convinced that this was him.

But Mr. Kapadia from the United States didn't make it to India, because he couldn't come during Diwali; so now he'd postponed his trip until the next year.

When Mummy heard the news, she complained to Pappa, "Once the boys go to America they think they're better than the rest of us. The American air leaves them as smug as maharajas. Is it right to announce that they're coming and then not show their faces? Do they ever think of what the poor girls and their parents must suffer through?"

"Are you saying that this Kapadia chap had no right to change his plans? What if he wasn't able to get leave from his work? What if he was sick? Should he feel guilty and come because a few anxious parents and their daughters are waiting for him?"

"Why can't he come after Diwali?"

"If the chap wants to come for Diwali, he should be able to come for Diwali. We didn't pay for his plane ticket, so how can we complain?"

"All I know is that when I look at Mohini I can't help but worry. And we're not done after Mohini. We have Jeeta to settle."

Foi was visiting us for a few days. She didn't seem too concerned about matchmaking for Mohini.

"Purnima, don't pay attention to my brother, *bhai*, and don't worry about Mohini. We were able to find a match for Nimita and this will be as easy as making a monkey dance," Foi said.

"Isn't it terrible that we waited for the groom from America and let so many others go? In the end we have nothing. And your *bhai* takes all this as light as water. "

"*Aaa su bole che?* What are you saying? Before this, we had no other chaps except the nephew of some Chaganlal Maganlal," Pappa said.

"Maganlal Chaganlal. Maganlal is a son of Chaganlal."

"Who cares if it's Maganlal Chaganlal or Chaganlal Maganlal? To me it makes no difference. And that fell from the sky because your cousin Kirti went and got her girl married. And good thing, too, for I wouldn't have approved of him in the first place."

"Why not?"

"Because he has no education."

"He is to inherit his uncle's business. What more do you need?"

"I don't need a boy. I need a man who can stand on his own two feet."

"Remember, people can snatch out of your hand, but never out of your kismet. I say Mohini will find whoever is her kismet," Foi said, getting up. She wouldn't tolerate any more arguments about the subject.

Discussions like this made me angry. Why couldn't Pappa and Mummy ever agree? I wondered. Mummy thought and lived the way her grandmother thought and lived, and Pappa—well, Pappa definitely thought differently from Mummy.

eight

THE DAY I met Mr. Judge, Sarina's pappa, will forever stay in my memory as the most bumbling-fumbling day of my life. It was Sarina's birthday, and she'd asked me to come for dinner. Her uncle and his family were also invited.

"But I've never even met your pappa, and now you want me to meet him *and* some other people," I protested.

"These are not just other people. They're my family. And didn't I come and meet six Parekhs and two Mehtas at one time? I don't remember protesting that there were too many."

I had no choice, and deep down I wanted to go even though I was shaky about how to greet them, what to talk about, how to eat, and when to smile. I fretted as if I'd never done those things in my life before.

Sarina's dinner was on a Saturday in December. After attending school from eight to eleven-thirty, I came home, ate lunch, and finished my homework. It was a beautiful afternoon. The early-morning chill had been driven away by sunshine, and the blue sky was dotted with kites.

At five I started getting ready to go to Sarina's house. Mohini let me wear her navy-blue silk *salwar-khameez*, a long shirt and baggy pants with a georgette *dupatta*, a scarf. On the front of the *khameez* were beautiful embroidered peacocks and two tiny ones on the sleeves. The *dupatta* was cream colored, with navy peacocks embroidered on it as well. Mohini braided my hair and added a small, creamy white rose that contrasted with my dark braid and matched my *dupatta*. I rimmed my eyes with kohl. Mohini picked out a navy pear-shaped *bindi* with a gold outline and placed it in the middle of my forehead. She even put lipstick on me.

As soon as Mummy saw me wearing lipstick, she told me to wipe it off. I didn't argue. The last thing I needed was for Mummy to get mad and stop me from going to the party.

The Princess Street area, where we lived, was always busy. All the taxis, cars, and buses kept honking their horns and only managed to creep along. I'd planned to take a bus, but when I got to the bus stop, the traffic was not moving at all. I had no idea what the problem was. Since Sarina's house was less than two miles away, I decided to walk.

When I got to Marine Lines Station I saw a crowd. I was concerned that there may have been a bad accident, but then I saw that people were laughing, clapping, whistling, and shouting cheerfully. Mummy always warned us to stay away from crowds. I shoved and wiggled my way through as quickly as I could.

Once I crossed the bridge and got to the other side, the footpaths were wide and empty, and I walked fast. It was exactly six-thirty when I rang the doorbell at Sarina's house. I had time to take one deep breath before Sarina opened the door and gave me a hug.

Mrs. Judge was sitting on a maroon-and-green-painted settee covered with a cushion the color of saffron-flavored milk. A couple was sitting across from her. Sarina introduced them as her uncle and aunt. Mrs. Judge motioned me to sit by her, and I was relieved.

"Pappa, Jeeta is here," Sarina called.

"We're here too," said a man with the same copper-colored complexion as Sarina, and dark, deep-brown eyes.

Ever since I'd found out that Sarina's pappa was a judge, I had imagined an imposing man in a huge black robe with a stern look. He didn't look like that at all. He was dressed in a white shirt with gray stripes, and gray trousers. He was not very tall, and definitely not very imposing.

Before I could get over the initial shock of meeting someone so different from the one I'd pictured, three boys walked in behind him, and the oldest of them was Neel.

Neel!

I almost tripped over my *dupatta* as I got up to greet the judge. Should I bend down and grab my *dupatta*, or greet him first? I wondered in a panic.

Mrs. Judge picked up the dupatta and put it over my shoulder and then wrapped her arm around me. My hands trembled so much that I could hardly say, "*Namaste.*"

Sarina introduced me to everyone and I must've mumbled something, but I couldn't remember anything. It was as if my mind were a big empty bowl that I cupped in my hand and stared at.

"Jeeta," the judge said as we sat down to eat. "I like the sound of your name. When I was a poor struggling lawyer I always thought about you."

Confused, I looked at him.

"Your name means 'victory,' doesn't it? Well, I wanted

to win the case I was fighting, so all day I would hum *jeeta, jeeta, jeeta.* I had no idea that a real Jeeta would walk into my house one day."

My ears turned red. The worst thing was that Neel was sitting right across from me and kept on eating spicy *batata vada,* potato balls. I wondered if Sarina knew that this was the same Neel, the one I'd told her I liked.

"How is college? Have you learned much in the past two years?" the judge asked Neel.

"Some."

"What do you mean, some? Don't tell me you've been cutting classes and going to movies like your pappa and I used to?"

"Did you do that, Pappa?" Neel asked.

"Jeeta, do I look like someone who would cut classes?" Neel's pappa asked me.

It was so unexpected that I couldn't even say, "no." My quick brain was not so quick after all.

"She thinks you're guilty as charged," Neel said.

I knew they were trying to make me comfortable, but I wished they'd forget I was there.

"Next year Sarina and Jeeta will be in college. Don't give them ideas," Mrs. Judge said.

"These kids don't need ideas from us," the judge said. Then he asked Neel what he wanted to do after he finished his college.

"I still have a couple of years to decide," he said. "I can finish my MBA here, or go to America and study there. Right now I'm in favor of staying here, but if I get a scholarship, I'll hop on a plane."

I thought, How can anyone so young be so confident in what he wants to do? Isn't he afraid of going to America by himself?

"Money shouldn't be the only consideration, Neel," the judge said. "When we were little your pappa and I strung beads by the thousands to make money to pay our school fees. When we were in college we used the streetlight by our house as our reading lamp. And now look where our struggles have brought us."

I realized Sarina's pappa and Neel's pappa were friends as well as brothers. No wonder they laughed and joked with each other.

"Pappa says the same thing, but like you and Pappa, I want to stand on my own feet."

"You'll not only stand, you'll fly," the judge said, beaming. "Sarina wants to be a doctor, just like her mummy. I can't seem to get her interested in studying law."

"One lawyer in the family, that's the rule," Mrs. Judge said.

"You don't want Sarina as a lawyer in your court," Neel's mummy said.

"Why not?"

"She'll make you forget you're a judge, that's why."

They all laughed. "Jeeta, what do you want to study?" Neel's pappa asked me.

"I . . . I have no idea."

"What's your favorite class?"

"History."

"Wasn't that your favorite subject too?" Sarina's aunt asked the judge.

"Yes. Maybe you'll want to pursue the law, Jeeta. Any lawyers in your family?"

I shook my head.

"Come see me if you want to go to law school."

I looked at Sarina. She knew how different and difficult this conversation was for me.

After dinner Sarina cut the cake. Mummy never allowed cake in our house because it contained eggs. I'd tasted tiny cakes from Iranian bakeries a few times. I loved those golden brown squares and rounds, frosted in pastel green and pink, cupped in crinkly tissue paper. There was never enough of it, though. Sarina's birthday cake was bigger than any I'd ever seen on display at the bakery store. Sarina's aunt had baked it, and it had no eggs in it. When I took a bite it reminded me of the December air blowing from the ocean, light and moist.

After the cake, Sarina opened her gifts. She picked up my package first and shook it. I was afraid that it would make noise and give away what was inside. I'd wrapped it in six layers of pink tissue paper before putting it in the box, and it made no sound. "Ah, silver anklets," she said when she opened it. "How did you know that I wanted a pair?"

"I always know what you want."

"And I know what you want," she said, her eyes dancing.

Her parents gave her an antique brass statue of Natraj, the dancing Shiva, surrounded by a whirling flame of cosmic energy, his right foot resting on the dwarf of spiritual ignorance.

Her aunt and uncle gave her a leather purse. Neel brought her the gift that I liked the best: a CD of *ghazals*, Urdu poetry.

It was nine-thirty when Sarina and I went to her room. "So, did you like my birthday party?" she asked.

"Oh, it was the best."

"See, you were panicky for no reason at all."

"I still am."

"Why, because Neel is here?"

"How did you know it was the same—"

"From the first time you talked about him I had this strange feeling, and then—"

"And then what?" Neel said, coming in. Sarina and I were sitting on her bed. Neel brought a wicker chair padded with a navy blue cushion close to us and plopped down.

I don't know what Sarina said. All I could think was Neel, Neel, and Neel. He was two feet away from me.

"You missed the last day of swimming. What happened?" Neel asked me.

"You remember that?"

"Yes. I was waiting for you and your smile; instead, there was your sister, who ignored me completely. I wanted to ask her about you, but I didn't have the courage."

"What? I never thought you were scared to talk to a girl," Sarina said.

"You would be, if you knew this one."

"Mohini is sweet. You could've talked to her," I said.

"Well, after she turned her face away how could I? What could I say?"

"At least you talked to Jeeta," Sarina said.

"You call that talking? I asked her maybe ten questions."

I looked straight into his eyes and said, "You could've asked more. I would've answered."

"Not when you sister was around and looked so annoyed."

"She was pretending not to notice anything."

"I see," Neel said, nodding as if all of a sudden he understood Mohini.

"What was Jeeta like?" Sarina asked.

"She wasn't quite as scary as her sister," Neel said. I raised my eyebrows at him. "Not scary at all."

The world was spinning through the whirl of a rainbow, and I was in the midst of it. Oh, how I wished I could stop time just enough to take one deep breath.

The judge came in and asked if we wanted to go for a walk. Sarina looked at me. "Do you want to go?"

"It's your birthday, you decide."

"Let's go," she said, pulling my and Neel's hands.

It was a typical December night: clear and crisp. The cars on Marine Drive were following a sleek curve, sliding past us smoothly. Mumbai's traffic in the inner city where I lived was always chaotic. No one stayed in their lanes or observed any rules. Handcarts and big trucks, and occasionally, a stray dog or a cow made the creeping traffic come to a total stop. On Marine Drive, at night, there were only cars, black-and-yellow cabs, and a few red double-decker buses going by.

The light turned green for us and we crossed the road. Except for some spicy-peanut, puffed-rice, and fried-lentil vendors, and a couple of sugarcane vendors, there were few people on the wide footpath.

Shimmering and swaying on the gentle waves, the four-day-old moon looked like a tiny *bindi* over the dark face of the Arabian Sea. Once in a while the breeze from the sea picked up, and I shivered. Neel must have noticed, because he took his cardigan off and wrapped it around my shoulders.

I shivered all over again to be so close to him.

"Are you still cold?" he asked as we walked a few more steps.

"No, I'm fine."

All of a sudden a wonderfully smoky smell filled the air. A young woman, her face glowing like gold sequins in the light of the burning coals, was roasting fresh corn on a *sagdi*. She was wearing a worn but beautifully embroidered mirror-work skirt and blouse. Her skirt covered her ankles but not her bare feet, and on each of her toes she wore a silver ring. As she rotated the cobs, the darkened kernels released a scent that was impossible to resist. We each ordered one and stood near the woman, warming up. After roasting the corn, she dipped a slice of lemon in salt and ground red pepper and rubbed it on each cob.

Neel, Sarina, and I took the cobs and sat on Marine Drive, while the rest of the family strolled on the footpath. Neel watched the waves as they gathered and crashed against the concrete blocks that had been put there to stop the ocean.

"Neel is hypnotized by the ocean," Sarina said.

"I am listening, I am eating, I am talking."

"I am singing, I am swaying, I am falling asleep," I said, mimicking Neel's tone.

Sarina laughed so loudly that a couple strolling by turned around.

"Let's walk," Neel said, and got up.

While we walked and ate, Neel continued to watch the ocean. He hardly said a word.

It didn't matter. I was swirling, twirling, furling in the rainbow.

Sarina and Neel brought me home at eleven. They waited in the car until I walked across the courtyard.

When I came into the apartment, Mummy said, "Look at her sailing in like a scented breeze."

Could she smell the perfume Sarina had sprayed on me? I wondered.

"I'm so tired," I said, and yawned.

"Go to sleep," Pappa said.

"Who brought you home?" Mummy asked.

"Sarina," I said, walking toward the bedroom.

"Who drove?"

I pretended I didn't hear.

"Probably her father did," Mummy answered herself.

I was relieved that the living room windows didn't face the main street and Mummy hadn't been able to see who had dropped me off.

As I lay on my mattress, I kept unfolding the last few hours over and over again.

Before I drifted to sleep I thought, when am I going to see Neel again?

nine

FOR THE PAST MONTH Mummy had been busy trying to find a match for Mohini. Mohini had even met two eligible boys, but neither went beyond the first meeting. Then a boy named Sunand came to see her. In his bio-data he'd mentioned that he'd received a gold medal for academic achievement.

"Why does Sunand have to mention the gold medal? He's not applying for a scholarship or looking for a job. What difference does it make?" I said to Mummy as I was tying my shoes.

"It does. It tells me he's smart and works hard."

"I suppose if Mohini gets married to him he'll have to get an extra-large turban for himself."

"Why?"

"To fit his oversize brain."

"If you don't stop making fun of him, I'll have to shrink your head."

I laughed as I slipped out the door.

Mummy had shown Mohini's and Sunand's horoscopes to a *pundit*, a scholar of Vedic philosophy, including astrology. After talking to him she was convinced Sunand and Mohini were going to get married. "The *pundit* says that thirty-three out of thirty-six points match. There'll never be a better match. This is it."

After the first meeting, Sunand and Mohini were both interested in each other. So they went out one evening. Mummy paced the bedroom. When the clock struck eight she said, "Gone for three hours! Soon, we might be eating brown sugar for good luck."

When Mohini came back she looked as pale as a raw banana and went straight to bed. The next morning when Mummy went to take her bath, Mohini and I were still in bed, pretending to be asleep.

Once I was certain that Mummy couldn't hear me, I asked, "How was Sunand?" We both sat up on our mattresses.

"I liked him the first time we met, when Mummy, Pappa, and Foi were with me. Last night, when it was only the two of us, he fired question after question at me as if he were an examiner."

"What did he ask you?"

"Everything! He asked me if I knew how to cook. When I said yes, he laughed and said, 'I don't mean the same, plain Gujarati food of dal, rice, and *rotli*. Do you know how to cook Punjabi food and South Indian food? Have you made pudding before? Do you know what a pizza is?'"

"Is he an incarnation of Bheem, from *Mahabharat*, or what, that all he could think about was food?"

She rested her face on her knees and wrapped her arms around her legs. She laughed faintly; then her eyebrows knitted again. "He did that with other things, too. He wanted to know what kind of marks I'd received in math and science. If I'd taken singing lessons. If I knew how to dance."

"You do *garba* and *dandia raas* so gracefully."

"I told him that I like folk dancing. He said what he meant by dance was the real classical dance, not moving in circles clapping your hands or banging your two sticks with your partner's."

"What did you say to that?"

"What could I? I kept quiet."

"I would've told him, '*Guruji*, my great teacher, if you can play classical music, I can tie brass bells on my ankles and dazzle you with my pirouettes and footwork of the *kathak* dance.' "

"I wish I could say those things," Mohini said.

"Don't wish. Just say them."

"I would if my brain worked as fast as yours. By the time I think of things to say, it is too late."

"My tongue is quicker than my brain. Sometimes it misfires and lands me on a pile of trouble. I wish I could just switch it off."

We heard the bathroom door opening. Mohini sat up straight and whispered, "I hope this circus ends soon."

"I thought getting you married would be the easiest of all. I suppose the prettier you are the fussier you are," Mummy said, when she found out that Mohini didn't want to marry Sunand.

Mohini shrugged.

"You must decide from the ones you meet, because no new ones are going to be born for you!"

I should've kept quiet but couldn't. "Mummy, this isn't like buying a sari that you can pick out from a stack. It's a question of a lifetime; let Mohini take her time."

"Don't be her lawyer. I want to know why she didn't like him."

"She just didn't."

"How do you know?"

"Because I'm like Narad Muni. I know the past, present, and future." Narad Muni was a sage in mythological stories. He played his *tambura*, a one-string instrument, traveled back and forth in time all across the universe, and meddled in everyone's business.

"Then it's time for you to visit some other planet and stir up things there."

"Let me—"

"I tell you, Jeeta, your tongue is too sharp and your color is too dark, so for your sake, when your time comes, say yes to the first man that says yes to you. Don't be fussy, and don't make your engagement a minute longer than it needs to be." Mummy's voice was loud and stiff, as if all the humor had drained out of it.

Mohini looked at me and then at Mummy. "I'll try to decide quickly. I will."

Mohini knew I was burning with anger, but she couldn't do or say anything for me. Mummy was always there. In the evening Mohini asked me to go out for sugarcane juice. There was a sugarcane juice stall right on the next street, but we decided to go farther away so that we wouldn't meet any of our neighbors. We crossed six streets before we reached the sugarcane stall. Except for the owner and one couple sitting on a long wooden bench,the place was empty. We sat on the opposite end of the bench from the couple and ordered two tall glasses of juice.

I liked this place because the owner, a man of Pappa's age, did all the work and kept it spotless.

"Are you still upset with Mummy?" Mohini asked.

"No. I deserved it for unleashing my tongue," I said as I watched the man pick out a couple of fresh canes, trim the ends off with a sharp knife, and pass them between the two moving wheels.

"You're still angry."

The man caught the canes coming out the other end, and once again passed them through, sticking in a piece of fresh gingerroot with each one. The frothy juice rolled down the gleaming, stainless steel half tunnel and into a big jug.

"I know Mummy hates my dark skin, but why does she assume that the rest of the world also finds it so offensive?"

"Mummy doesn't hate it. She's worried about our future and happiness, that's all."

Quickly, the man poured the juice into glasses, squeezed half a lemon into each, and handed them to us, before a single one of the hustling flies had time to land on them. When he left I said, "You keep saying that, but I don't believe it. It seems like we're clutter that she wants to get rid of."

"Please, try and understand Mummy. Do you realize that she worried about Nimita constantly? It drained so much energy out of her. Now she wants to find good husbands for us and wants us to be happy, too."

"But I don't like the way she's doing it. She's pressuring you to say yes quickly, before you even know the person. In a way, Nimita had less to worry about. Most men said no to her before she had a chance to decide, but it's different for you. And I dread the time she starts looking for me. Maybe Mummy wants us to be happy, but in the process she's making us miserable. I know she loves us, but I still wonder."

I took a long sip while Mohini talked.

"Don't forget the old saying, 'A mother is a mother, and the rest of the people are breezes that blow from the jungle.'"

I sucked up the last of my juice and set my glass to the side. "When your own mother suffocates you, a breeze from the jungle might feel good."

"It's difficult enough for me without you arguing with her and about her. Believe me, if the next person I meet is halfway decent, you'll be next. Then you can do whatever pleases you," she said, swirling her glass and looking at the last of the sweet, brownish juice.

I wanted to say so much to her, but I didn't know where to begin.

ten

IN JANUARY, Foi came to stay with us for a month to help prepare for Mohini's wedding with Anoop. Even though Anoop was not a magistrate's son, he'd come from America, and Mummy had read about him in the matrimonial column. The only thing we knew about his family was that Anoop's mother had passed away a year ago and that his father was a bank officer who was going to retire in a year and then go live with his son in America.

I suppose before Anoop's father could go to America he needed a good *bahu*, a wife for Anoop, who could cook, clean, and keep his name going.

After meeting Mohini only once, Anoop said he was interested. The next day he canceled his appointment to meet another girl and took Mohini out instead.

Things moved faster than any of us could've imagined. The *pundit* read Mohini's and Anoop's horoscopes and said that they matched well. He also gave us a few auspicious dates for the marriage ceremony. Anoop's father said yes, too, and so Mohini had to decide right away. I knew she wanted more time with Anoop and also more time before she made her decision, but it never happened. Mummy was not going to let such a fine young man get away.

"Once you let go of the matter, he might go and see other girls, and then where will you be? If you don't have anything against him then let's have an instant engagement and a quick wedding," Mummy told Mohini one morning while she, Pappa, and Foi were having their second cup of tea.

"But we hardly know anything about Anoop. How do we know he's the right person?" I asked.

"We know enough about him," Mummy said. "He's from our caste, he's educated, and he lives in America. Mohini will have a good life with him."

"Anoop seems like the right match for Mohini," Foi said. "I wish we had more time, but when a boy comes for a short while from far away, we have to decide fast."

"Anoop is a stranger. None of our relatives or friends even know him. What if he makes Mohini miserable?"

"Why do you utter terrible words? He's a *Modh Bania*, from the same caste as us, and that's all we need," Mummy said.

"But Fua isn't from our caste and Foi married—"

"*Choop ker!* Have you pawned your manners? Small mouths mustn't talk big talks. This isn't about your marriage, so sit on the side and shut your mouth tight," Mummy said.

I looked at Pappa, but he didn't say a word. I knew we never discussed why Fua wasn't from our caste, and it was a mistake for me to talk about it, especially in front of Foi.

"If Mohini is ready, let's announce the engagement. Do you agree, Mohini?" Mummy asked.

Mohini nodded, and her engagement to Anoop was fixed. That day Pappa was quiet and serious, as if he were calculating a complicated math problem in his head. I wished he would take me for a walk after dinner, but he asked Mohini to go with him instead. Mummy wanted Chiraj to join them, but Pappa said, "Before I send Mohini far away, let me spend a few moments with her alone."

The next day congratulations flooded in from relatives, neighbors, and friends. If Mohini was overwhelmed by all this, no one suspected it. At the engagement gathering she looked like an *apsara*, a celestial dancer, in her purple sari with a pink brocade border.

"You're so lucky! A chance to live in America is as good as marrying a millionaire," Kirti Auntie said.

"Yes, you never know what our kismet brings us," Mummy replied. She hadn't forgiven Kirti Auntie for digging up the information on the nephew of Mr. Maganlal Chaganlal and quickly arranging Jayshree's engagement with him.

"Yes, yes, you're absolutely right. Mohini's karma must take her far away from home. I, for one, wouldn't want Jayshree living in a strange country, but you have three, so you can easily send one away," she said.

Jayshree and her husband, Mr. Maganlal Chaganlal's nephew, were both there. I was annoyed when she laughed out loud, throwing her head back, and clinging to her husband's hand as if she were his extra appendage.

Mummy couldn't say a word. I knew she wanted to, but Kirti Auntie was a few months older than Mummy, so Mummy had to swallow insults like that and keep on smiling. Mohini had tears in her eyes, so I dragged her away from the group. When Foi heard about what Kirti Auntie had said, she shook her head and said, "I wonder where Kirti was when God sprinkled sense on us all."

"Do you like Anoopji?" I whispered to Mohini that night.

"He thinks adding *ji* behind a name is old-fashioned. He wants you to call him Anoop."

"Fine. Was Anoop nice?"

"Yes. He picked out a rose from the flower shop for me. When I asked what I should do with it, he said, 'If you allow me, I'll put it in your hair.' And then when he brought me home he asked if he could take the rose with him. I said, 'What are you going to do with a wilted rose?' He said, 'It's not a wilted rose. It's filled with the fragrance of your hair.' "

"It sounds like dialogue straight out of a Bollywood movie."

"I think it's romantic."

In the dark I couldn't see Mohini's face, but her voice sounded soft and dreamy. She was happy and I didn't want to blow out her dreams, but I thought his words sounded made up. Was he an actor who had rehearsed the scene a few times before performing it for Mohini? I wondered.

Anoop had only three weeks off, and so the marriage had to take place quickly. The marriage was fixed on one of the auspicious dates that the *pundit* had given us, only ten days after Mohini and Anoop's engagement. Again, as the bride's family, we had to arrange for the hall, the priest, the dinner, and the flowers. With Foi's help, Mummy managed everything.

Mohini's wedding preparation took a lot of my time. I saw Sarina at school, but I couldn't go to her house. I missed sitting on the balcony watching the waves, the ocean breeze ruffling my hair. I missed talking with Sarina, and seeing Neel.

While I was helping Mummy with the invitations, I saw a list of special people to whom we were personally going to deliver them. When I saw Sarina's name on it, a brilliant idea smiled upon me.

"Can I go to Sarina's house this Sunday?" I asked.

"The house of a wedding is like a house of bees. Mohini is queen, but you're not. I need your help. We have a list of people that we have to hand deliver the invitations to."

"Mummy, you'd better go to Kirti Auntie's house first; otherwise she'll be offended."

"She's first on my list. We should also go to Sarina's house to invite her family."

"Sarina's family?" I said, as if I were surprised. "When you go to Kirti Auntie's house, I can go to Sarina's house."

Mummy rested her hand on her chin. "I don't know. How would it look if Pappa or I didn't go with you to invite them?"

"You don't have time. Besides, they won't mind if I go alone. Kirti Auntie and all our other relatives would."

"Yes. Tell them how sorry Pappa and I are for not being able to come. Tell them how much we want them to come to the wedding."

"I will."

At school I told Sarina I was going to visit her on Sunday. She asked, "Can you stay for lunch?"

"No, I can't."

"I'll ask Neel, too."

"You're tempting me."

"That's the idea."

"Somehow, I'll have to convice Mummy," I mumbled.

On Sunday, I dressed up in a chiffon silk *salwar-khameez* and opal earrings, to deliver the invitation to Sarina's house.

The judge opened the door and raised his eyebrows, "Are you sure you want to come to our place dressed up like this?"

"Why? What's wrong?' I looked at myself, wondering if I'd forgotten my *dupatta* at home.

"You look like a pink lotus. You should be surrounded by blue water."

Why did I always get flustered when Sarina's pappa or uncle teased me? Why couldn't I come up with a witty response?

"Pappa, if you give Jeeta a hard time, she won't invite you to the wedding," Sarina said as she walked into the living room.

"Is Jeeta getting married?"

"Don't talk about Jeeta's marriage yet. She's going to become a lawyer first," Mrs. Judge hollered. She was watering her bonsai plants on the balcony.

I handed the judge their invitation. "Mummy wanted to come, but we have so little time to prepare."

"We're glad you're here," the judge said.

"Come in my room," Sarina said. Her eyes were darting, dancing, as if she couldn't wait to tell me something.

I waited until the judge and Mrs. Judge read the invitation. "We'll be there," Mrs. Judge said.

"Mummy and Pappa will be happy," I said.

Sarina stood there tapping her foot.

"Go, go," the judge said. "Sarina can't wait to tell you about a boy she met yesterday."

"Who did I meet?"

"Didn't you? Maybe you'll meet him today."

"Sure, Pappa."

"What boy?" I asked as soon as we were in her room.

"No one. Pappa's teasing me because I couldn't wait to talk to you."

"Oh!"

She sat down crossed-legged on her bed, hugging a pillow. "Neel and I were wondering if you could go on a picnic, just the three of us."

"I don't know if Mummy will say yes."

"Why not? It'll be after the wedding. Ask her. We're planning to go to Vihar Lake, so it'll take a while to get there. If we leave by nine-thirty we'll have a full day there. I promise you complete fun for your time."

Sarina was so excited that I hated to remind her, but I did anyway, "I still have to ask Mummy. I'll call you."

"Make sure she says yes."

"Are you ready for lunch?" Mrs. Judge called. "Neel will be here any minute."

While we were eating, the judge asked Neel, "Are you staying for a while?"

"Yes, I am."

"Then let's play cards. That way we won't bother these two girls. They have a lot to talk about."

"Um . . . cards? With you? I suppose."

Sarina and I gave each other a look. It was impossible not to laugh.

Half an hour after the lunch, Neel managed to get away from the judge, and came to Sarina's room.

"So did you let Pappa win?"

"I had to."

"Pappa only quits playing after he wins," Sarina explained to me.

Neel picked up my *dupatta*, which was dragging on the floor to one side.

"This shade looks good on you," he said, fingering the cloth.

"Thanks."

For the next few minutes Sarina rattled off details about the picnic. I tried to listen to what she was saying while Neel played with my *dupatta*. It was as if he were tugging at my heart, and I couldn't concentrate on anything else.

When I looked at my watch I realized I'd been away for too long. I hurried home, thinking about Neel. There was no other choice but to convince Mummy to let me go to the picnic.

As soon as I got home I rushed to ask Mummy if I

could go with Sarina. "An all-day picnic in the middle of the wedding?"

"No, no, after Mohini and Anoop leave for their honeymoon. Please, Mummy, let me go. I've never been there. It'll be fun to spend a day with my friends."

Mummy was quiet for a while and then she looked up and asked, "Who is going?"

"Sarina."

"Who else? You said friend*s*."

"Maybe her Mummy and Pappa."

"Since when did they become your friends?"

I knew that if Mummy suspected that Neel was also going, she'd never let me out of the house. As I fumbled for an answer, she said, "First, find out who's going with her. Even by car I won't allow the two of you to go that far alone. Did you deliver the invitation?"

"Yes, and they said they'll all come."

"The judge too?"

"Yes, the judge, the doctor, and their daughter."

Mummy smiled. "I suppose you can go to Vihar Lake with them."

"Thanks, Mummy," I said, and gave her a bear hug.

* * *

The next day Sarina came late to school. By the time she'd settled in, class had begun. "Neel wants to know, can you go?" she whispered.

"What are you two talking about?" Mrs. Kailas said. Besides Hindi, she taught us history and geography.

"I . . . I didn't say a word," I stuttered.

"All right, if you were paying attention, what independence movement were we talking about?"

My mind turned as dark as a cave. I looked down and saw "*Bharat Chhodo*, Quit India," which Sarina had written in big bold letters in her notebook.

"*Bharat Chhodo.*"

"Good, and Sarina, what were you whispering to Jeeta? And don't deny it. I saw it with my own eyes."

"Really?" someone whispered from the back. "I thought she rented her eyes."

Sarina heard the comment, but with a straight face said, "I was telling Jeeta about something she likes." Two girls sitting behind us began giggling. It was easy for them to figure out that we must have been talking about a boy.

"Share with us what Jeeta likes," Mrs. Kailas insisted. Most of the time, I hated the idea of an all-girls school, and yet, at times like this, I was happy that there were no boys in the classroom.

Sarina looked at me and took a deep breath. I lowered my eyes. Maybe it had something to do with her father being a judge, because Sarina never lied.

"What she likes comes from my father's side of the family and is quite unique. I'd seen Jeeta with such an admirable longing for it when she came to my house that I thought maybe she would . . . not that I have permission or a right to give her what she desires without the consent of others. I was asking her—"

"All right, all right, that's enough," Mrs. Kailas said, with a sweeping motion of her hand. "You may sit down."

At recess Yamini said, "Promise you'll bring Neel's picture tomorrow."

"I don't have his picture," I said.

"I'm asking Sarina."

"Take a picture of Jeeta and Neel together. Make them hold hands," Janki said.

"Hold hands? Are you in the middle of the fifth century? Can't you think of a more romantic pose than that?" Yamini said. Then she whispered something in Janki's ear. Janki covered her mouth with her hands as if she didn't want those words to spill out of her mouth.

That afternoon half of the class asked Sarina what it was that I liked so much. She merely smiled mysteriously.

eleven

WE DIDN'T have to give as much to Anoop as we had to Girishji. Even when Mohini bought clothes, jewelry, and other personal things, Anoop said, "Don't buy too much, Mohini. Indian things and Indian ways are of no use there. Once we get to America we'll shop for your clothes."

One day Mummy, Mohini, and I went out to Shyama to buy saris for Mohini—a fancy place on Marine Drive that had the latest fashions in saris and dress materials. That morning the shop was relatively empty, and we sat on padded stools in front of a glass counter. A gentleman with more gray than black hair clinging to his scalp stood behind the counter and asked us what we wanted. When we told him we were looking for saris for the bride, he was pleased. Those were the most expensive saris.

He looked at Mummy and asked, "For which one of them?"

"For her," I replied, pointing to Mohini.

"*Saras, saras*, good, good."

I think he was relieved that it was not for me. Just like Mummy, he was probably wondering, With such dark skin, what color would look good on her? It would be easy to find a sari for Mohini. Everyone thought so. Mohini's sandalwood-colored skin was such a perfect shade that all colors looked good on her.

One after another, the man began to spread saris on the counter. They were beautiful: a bloodred chiffon with heavy gold-thread embroidery; an ink-blue, handwoven silk with silver sequins; and a parrot-green organza with a wide gold-and-silver border.

"I want something simpler," Mohini said.

"For a wedding and a reception, this is the fashion; this is what all the brides are wearing," he said, spreading one of the saris on his shoulder.

"That sari looks good on you," I said to the salesman.

"*Choop ker,*" Mummy said.

"Sorry, I meant the lavender color."

"Don't be sorry. This is an everyday thing for me.

I'd rather wear lavender over red any day—look," he said, folding the red sari over a shoulder while holding up the lavender one. "Isn't this beadwork beautiful? It'll look lovely with gold jewelry."

Mohini shook her head. "These are too heavy."

"If this is what everyone is wearing these days then you'd better buy the same things. Otherwise, it'll look inappropriate," Mummy said.

I knew that Mummy was worried people might think that she and Pappa hadn't spent enough money on Mohini's sari.

"Anoop said that very heavy saris are of no use in America. If it's a simple one then I can wear it on other occasions, too."

Anoop's name was enough for Mummy to be quiet, but not for the salesman. He said, "You only get married once. Buy the best for the reception." He opened up a peacock-blue sari and draped it over his shoulder for us to see. "Just this morning a girl came and bought the same piece in purple. She's going to New Jersey. Are you going to New Jersey or New York?"

"Illinois," Mohini said.

He was mumbling "Illinois, Illinois," when I said, "Please, Uncle, show us a few simple ones."

I'd asked him so politely and sweetly that he couldn't refuse. He swept all the opened saris down the counter and took out a pile of silk chiffon saris. A young assistant began folding all the heavy saris that had piled up.

The salesman opened one sari after the other. The fabrics were soft and the colors vivid, but the gold work was done sparingly. "I like these," Mohini said. "Elegant yet simple."

Mohini and I were absorbed in looking at the saris while Mummy talked to the salesman. "The girls don't listen to us anymore." Mummy sighed. "It was different in our time. When I got married I didn't buy one single new sari. My mother had collected saris over a period of two years, and that's what I got. Fashion, bashion—it didn't matter. I was glad to have those saris. Nowadays, children are so fussy."

"We didn't dare ask about anything of our choice," he replied. "Not even who we married. If we did, we got our ears twisted so hard that we forgot what we wanted."

I asked him, "Uncle, in the very old times, women like Damyanti and Kunti in *Mahabharat* chose their own husbands. Don't you think we should go back to that tradition?"

I'd trapped him. He shook his head as if to break loose.

Good thing Mummy was asking Mohini something and hadn't heard what I said.

We selected three saris, two for Mohini and one for me. Uncle was pleased, and he ordered orange-flavored Fanta for us. While he made the bill, we sipped our drinks. "I am sure this one brings you much joy," he said, glancing at me first and then at Mummy, his glasses dangling halfway down the slope of his nose.

"Joys and headaches both. She can be as sweet as a mango and as sharp as a tiger's tooth," Mummy replied.

Anoop, I must admit, was certainly not as good-looking as Girishji, yet his manners were charming. He spoke fluent English with an American accent. His thin face and deep-set eyes made him look as though he hadn't eaten a good meal in two years. I knew that if he stayed here and ate with Girishji every Sunday, his face would fill out in no time. His black hair was wavy and coarse.

The first thing I whispered to Sarina at the wedding was, "I hope and pray that their children will inherit their mummy's hair."

"Let's not take any chances. I'll pray too," she said with a straight face and serious tone. Then we both burst out laughing.

Mohini's wedding was a hurried, chaotic celebration. It was like gulping down *ladu* without savoring a bite. Later I wondered if it had really happened. Now that Mummy had found one foreign-living *jamai*, son-in-law, she was determined to find another. She asked Anoop if he had any single friends from our caste living in America. I knew that was for me.

Only a few years ago I thought that a girl should marry before she was twenty-one or twenty-two. Mummy had married when she was nineteen, Nimita at twenty-one, and Mohini at twenty. Now that idea had washed out of my head completely, and there was no way it was going to get back in.

The morning after the wedding, Pankaj Kaka, Hema Auntie's husband, poked his head in the living room. "Two down and one to go. And this time you hit a sixer with Mohini," he said, swinging an imaginary cricket bat.

"Yes, with God's wishes we've found such a good *jamai*," Mummy said, looking up at Lord Krishna's picture. "Please, have some tea."

"I never say no to a good cup of tea," Pankaj Kaka said, lowering himself onto the divan. He was not a huge man, but his stomach was the roundest of rounds you could ever imagine, and when he laughed at his own comments it bobbed like a coconut in the ocean.

"You're next," he said as I handed him a cup of tea. I gave him a stare icier than the winds from the Himalayas.

"She still has a few years," Pappa said. "She is doing well in her studies. I'd like her to study law or medicine."

Pankaj Kaka's mouth sagged with surprise. He'd thought that I wasn't a very good student. "Daughters are never your own, and unlike sons, you have to part with them. It's better to get them married at a young age and be done with your responsibilities," he said, blowing on his tea to cool it.

"Nonsense," Pappa said. "My daughters are no burden to me. I want to see them happy just like I want to see Chiraj and Vivek happy. I see no difference between Jeeta and Chiraj."

"You can't mean that," Pankaj Kaka said, after taking a big gulp of tea and wiping his lips and mustache with his hand. "Chiraj and Vivek are your sons! They'll live with you the rest of your life, and your daughters only till they're married. Surely, Purnima will see that Jeeta is married in a few years. And I am with Purnima on this one. The sooner you get Jeeta settled in her life the sooner you can achieve peace of mind."

"Why do I have to be married to be considered settled?" I said.

"Because once you're married your parents' responsibilities are over."

"If I find a good match for Jeeta tomorrow, I'll have her married tomorrow," Mummy said.

"Purnima, you can't be serious." Pappa's voice shook.

Mummy didn't answer.

I was still standing there, but I wished I'd gone in the bedroom five minutes ago. Pankaj Kaka looked as though he were trapped between the two. Pappa always said, "Pankaj changes his views like a servant of a British officer: quickly, flatteringly, and without conviction."

Seeing Pappa's mood, Pankaj Kaka tried to calm the argument. "I think what Purnima is saying is, that if a good proposal like Mohini's comes by for Jeeta too, she'd certainly consider it."

"Mohini was ready to get married. Good horoscope match or not, I told her unless she was sure, she didn't have to get married," Pappa said.

"You did, Pappa?" The words sprang from my mouth. I didn't know that Pappa had ever talked to Mohini about her marriage. I had a special relationship with Pappa. I talked too boldly and he encouraged and enjoyed me, but I had no idea that Mohini talked to him too.

"I must get going," Pankaj Kaka said, looking at his watch and trying to trot out as gracefully as a camel.

On Sunday after Anoop and Mohini went to Matheran, a vacation place on the hills of the Western Ghatts near Mumbai, for their honeymoon, I went on the picnic with Neel and Sarina.

As soon as we entered the park surrounding the lake, the temperature dropped several degrees. The stately neem, the tall *kesuda*, and the wide banyan trees fanned us. Some of the mango trees were still in bloom and others were full of finger-long mangoes. The tiny mangoes swayed when the slightest breeze tickled them. Soon, these mangoes will swell so big they'll dangle lazily, I thought.

"Shhh . . . *choop*," Neel said, putting his finger to his mouth. We heard a sweet *koo-hoo, koo-hoo*, coming from the tree.

"A koyal?" I whispered. Neel nodded.

It wasn't the first time I'd heard a koyal singing, but it was the first time I'd heard one with Neel. We stood there quietly, and after a few seconds, Neel pointed. "Look, there, black koyal."

Seeing the black koyal singing on a tree branch sent a happy tingle through my heart.

After an hour of strolling, Neel and I sat down in the grassy shade of a neem tree. Sarina walked over to the playground. The tree murmured as the cool breeze coming off the lake played with its leaves.

What if Mummy finds out about this? What will she do? I shuddered at the thought.

Neel asked, "What's bothering you, Jeeta?"

"Nothing," I said, picking up a branch of ferny leaves from the neem tree.

"What is it?"

"It's just that . . . I didn't tell Mummy that the three of us were going together."

"Your mummy doesn't even know I exist."

"I know, and . . ." I said, twisting the leaves around my fingers. A smell of bitter neem filled the air. I flung the branch as far as I could.

"And?"

"And Mummy wouldn't allow me to go to Sarina's house if she knew that Sarina had a cousin who came over. When she found out that Yamini had two older brothers it was settled. I could be Yamini's friend at school, but I could never visit her at home."

"I don't want to cause any problems for you at home, and I certainly don't want your friendship with

Sarina to suffer because of me," Neel said, looking away.

My heart tore when he looked away. "Oh, no. It. . . . It's just that if Mummy finds out about us and stops me from visiting . . . please understand." My throat was all dry and I could barely finish the sentence.

"Of course," he said, putting his arm around me and pulling me closer. I put my head on his shoulder.

For a short time the fear that had prowled through my head abated.

After lunch, while we were strolling, we gathered and washed tiny green mangoes that had fallen from the tree. We ate them after dipping them in salt and red pepper that Sarina had brought. Some were so sour they turned my mouth inside out.

"Here's the parrot's nest," Neel said, when we were under the canopy of a tree. I looked up in the branches but didn't see a nest anywhere.

"Where?"

"It's right there," Sarina said, pointing.

I looked way up to the top and still couldn't see a thing.

Neel took my face in his hands and moved it down. "It's right on the trunk. See the hole there?"

I saw the nest—and I felt his hands on my cheeks for the rest of the day.

twelve

IN THE HEAT OF APRIL and May, Matheran was crowded, but not in early February. While Mohini was gone, I wondered if she was getting to know Anoop better. I wondered if she was happy with him, if she had any regrets about marrying him so quickly.

When they returned I wanted to talk to her, but there was no time since Anoop was leaving in three days and stayed as attached to Mohini as if he were one end of her sari.

I wanted to enjoy a few more days with her, talk to her, and maybe tell her about Neel, so I was glad Mohini's visa hadn't come and she couldn't go with Anoop right away.

The day after Anoop left for America, Mohini and I were alone in the house listening to a tape that

Anoop had given her. We tried to listen to the words, but all we could hear was loud music.

"I don't understand a word of it," Mohini said, turning the tape off.

From one of our neighbors' radios, Lata's voice floated, "*Koo hoo, koo hoo, bole koyal-ia,*" When the song was over, I said, "Tell me all about Anoop."

She glanced at me. There was something in her eyes that made me shiver. It was the same look she had when Mummy had shouted at us when we were little and we huddled together trying to comfort each other.

"What?" I asked, squeezing her hand.

"Nothing." She looked away. "In Matheran, Anoop was so attentive and romantic, asking me where I'd like to go first in America. When we passed through a small tunnel called the 'one-kiss tunnel,' he kissed me quickly but softly. It was so perfect, I was afraid."

"Afraid? Afraid of what?"

"That an evil stare would spoil my happiness."

"When did you become so superstitious? You have nothing to worry about."

"I hope you're right," she whispered.

"Your wedding, Anoop—it all feels like a movie. I can

see the wedding, I can picture Anoop, but only from a distance."

"It all happened so fast that even to me it feels like a dream. Anoop said the same thing."

A few days later Mohini got a call for her visa, and as she packed her bags, she seemed to be deep in thought. I teased her, saying, "You are meditating on Anoop."

She just shook her head. A tear rolled down her cheek. She gave me a hug and said, "I'll miss you so much."

"And I will miss you."

For the next few days I spent as much time as I could with Mohini and soaked up memories like the earth soaks up rain. I knew that by the time Mohini returned, I'd be as parched as the summer earth waiting for the monsoon rain.

One evening Mohini and I climbed all the steps to her favorite Shiva temple at Babulnath. The beggars, mostly old men and women in rags, were sitting on both sides of the steps, and Mohini dropped some change into their aluminum bowls. That was her money that she'd decided to give away before she left.

Right outside the temple, we took our sandals off and gave them to a shoe keeper, a boy no more than ten years old with sun-bleached, dusty brown hair. His eyes were bright.

He tucked our sandals into one of the cubicles under his bench. The marble under our bare feet was cool. Mohini smiled when I rang one of the big brass bells twice, once for her and once for me.

Flowers and burning incense filled the air as I closed my eyes and recited *Shiva Stotra*, a prayer. We walked out, tipped the shoe keeper, and right away he grabbed our sandals from the cubicle. He was a smart boy who remembered which shoes belonged to whom and which cubicles he'd kept them in. I knew he'd do well in school if he had the chance.

We sat down on the bench to fasten our straps. From the top of the hill we could see the ocean on one side and the city on the other. Mohini looked all around and sighed. "I don't know when I'll be back here again."

"Soon. It's always sooner than you think." Right there I wanted to tell Mohini about Neel, but I wasn't sure what she would think. I decided not to mention him.

That night Mohini gave me her set of four books written by Munshi. They were historical fiction set in Gujarat a thousand years ago. "Why are you giving them to me? You should take them with you."

"I can't. There are more important things for me to take than books."

"Certainly not more important. Only more practical."

"Maybe," she said. "Once I go, you may want to read them again."

I opened the first book. Inside, Mohini had written:

At the edge of an ocean, the past is carved on the stone, and the future lies deep under the water. Only the present we write and wipe in the sand of time.

For Jeeta,
With whom I've shared the beach and the sand of my childhood.

I held Mohini close.

Unlike Mummy, I didn't cry at the Chhatrapati Shivaji International Airport or even when we rode home in the taxi. At three in the morning, the city was silent, and so was I. I gazed out the window. The salty air filled my lungs as we drove by the Verli Sea-Face. When we passed the Haji Ali Dargah, I knew that Mohini was going to miss us; she was going to miss Mumbai; she was going to miss India.

The open ground of the Race Course stretched out on the opposite side of the road. We had never walked on the meandering rocky path that led to the Haji Ali Dargah, or seen a horse race on Sunday afternoons, and yet, how many times had we passed the cluster of ethereal white domes of Dargah floating on the water, or admired the open space of the Race Course? During the wedding season, rich people held their big weddings and receptions on the Race Course, and the trees were all aglow with lights and festivity.

I wondered how many years, months, days, and nights would pass until we brought Mohini home, passing right by this very same road? How happy I'd be on that day, talking to her and not noticing anything around us. But tonight I saw it all.

Our servant Naran had made up the beds, and as soon as we got home, Mummy told Chiraj, Vivek, and me to go to sleep. I lay down on my mattress. Tonight, there was only one mattress—only my mattress with two pillows stacked up on one end. I don't know why Naran gave me Mohini's pillow too.

When Mummy turned the lights off, I hugged Mohini's pillow tightly. I was surrounded by so much empty room that I felt a lump rising within me. I reached out my hand to see if I could feel Mohini, if I could just touch her and whisper something to her. She'd been with me for all these years, and maybe I could still make her be there. But in one night she was gone, and all the years of habit, love, desire, or imagination couldn't bring her back.

The lump rested in my throat and mixed with the salty air I breathed. I cried myself to sleep. When I woke up, the pillowcases were smeared with black kohl.

After Mohini left, Mummy kept sighing, "When a daughter leaves, your heart pricks." I noticed Mummy wiping her eyes with the end of her sari when she thought no one was looking. The pricking of her heart and her sadness surprised me, but I was too busy getting ready for my finals to give it much thought.

thirteen

NOW I HAD to catch up on my studies. Because Foi had come for two weeks in January for the wedding, she wouldn't be coming back to stay and help me prepare for my tests like she usually did; I had to study on my own. I was worried about that, but something unexpected happened. It was as if a gift had blown in through the window. One day, Mummy said, "It might be good for you to study with Sarina. You know, two can undertake a task better than one."

"Oh!"

"She may come over any time."

"With so many of us, it'll be hard for Sarina to concentrate. She's not used to it," I said.

"Then maybe you can go to her house, and if it's fine with her family, you can stay the night, too."

I danced inside, but I dared not show my delight. "I'll talk to her," I said, and continued to read about the battle of Paniput.

I packed for Sarina's house for the weekend as if I were going on a grand vacation. Since I had a pair of green-and-gold dangling earrings, I selected cotton *salwar-khameez* in the palest shade of green, with a matching *dupatta* to wear with it. It was one of my best everyday outfits. Mohini had let me have one of her perfumes. Its scent had a soothing, evocative feel to it, as if fragrant flowers were mixed with *ghazals*. I took that with me.

On Friday night Sarina and I studied for Saturday's assignment and then went to bed early. After lunch on Saturday afternoon Mrs. Judge said, "Don't forget we're going to Uncle's house for dinner."

My heart jumped.

"Not me," I said, hoping I was invited.

"You are too."

"I'm not family. Are you sure they want me to come?"

"Of course they want you to come."

I got my wish, but I wasn't ready for it.

For the rest of the afternoon, while Sarina and I sat there doing math, my mind wandered away. Sarina was so engrossed in her studies that she hadn't noticed that I'd yawned and stretched a dozen times. I wondered how she could find solving math problems so interesting on a Saturday afternoon. For me, it had been a long, long day.

Because I hadn't packed any dress clothes, Sarina insisted I wear one of her outfits that evening. In school we both wore the same uniform: a white blouse and khaki jumper. Her regular clothes, however, were different from mine. Most of hers were ready-made, bought at fancy shops, while mine were stitched by a tailor in a shop that was as big as Sarina's closet. She gave me her black skirt and cream-colored silk blouse, and tied my hair back in a fancy palm-tree braid.

"I wish I had your complexion," she said.

"Mine?" I said, pointing to myself.

"Yes, yours."

"But I'm so dark."

"So? Your skin is so dark, smooth, and glossy."

"Are you sure it's not just oily?"

"It isn't, and you know it. Isn't she pretty, Mummy?" she asked Mrs. Judge, who had just walked into her room.

"Jeeta is beautiful."

I could feel my ears turning red. Me, beautiful? People, including my family, had always said good things about my eyes, my sharp features, or my posture, but I knew they all felt that I was too dark to be beautiful. That evening, when I sprayed a little perfume and wore my green-and-gold earrings, I felt pretty—something I'd never felt before, even when I had dressed up for my sisters' weddings.

Neel and his family lived only a mile from Sarina's. When we arrived, Neel wasn't home. It was half an hour before the sunset, so we sat out in the balcony, where we could see Chowpatty Beach and the ocean. It was a warm day and the beach was crowded. Unlike the night of Sarina's birthday, today there were many vendors combing the area.

The entire row of *bhel-puri wallahs*, with their carts, stood busily selling savory mixtures of lentil noodles, puffed rice, and potatoes drenched in hot and sweet-and-sour chutney. Just the thought of *bhel-puri* made my mouth water.

I kept glancing at the front door. Sarina must have noticed and asked, "Where's Neel? Isn't it rude of him not be here when he knew we were coming, Jeeta?"

All eyes turned to me. I shrugged my shoulders. "If you miss him, call him."

Sarina's eyes widened. "I suppose I will."

"It's getting late. Let's eat," Sarina's aunt said, standing up. Everyone followed her except Sarina and me.

Right then Neel opened the door and rushed in. He was out of breath and his thick hair was flying about.

"Bless you. You have a long life. Sarina was talking about you only a minute ago," Mrs. Judge said.

"Oh, no," he said, walking toward us. "I know Sarina; she must have been complaining about me, wasn't she, Jeeta?"

"At least I missed you. Jeeta was perfectly content without you," Sarina said.

"Is she telling the truth?" he asked, touching my right shoulder. A surge of electricity ran down my spine.

I clasped my hands together. "I was content before and I'm content now."

"My presence means nothing to you?"

"I didn't say that."

"You're implying it, isn't she, Sarina?" he asked.

Sarina was no longer there. "Where did she go?" I wondered aloud.

"And when?"

Then we both started laughing.

The western sky over the water had turned to shades of oleander, and the sun was just about to set. In the glow, Neel's hair turned pomegranate and his skin turned to molten gold. I sat there letting his midnight eyes mesmerize me.

"Time to eat," Sarina called to us. Dark had descended on the beach except for the lamps that lit the food carts.

Tonight, as if Neel's family had read my mind, they served *bhel-puri*. We piled up our plates and walked back to the veranda. The stars were coming out and the smell from a *raatrani*, night-blooming jasmine, became intense. The fragrance of *raatrani*, the smell of spicy food, and the racing of my own heart made me giddy.

"Can the five of us go to the beach?" Sarina asked after dinner.

"Sure," Mrs. Judge said.

It was late and the crowds had thinned out on the beach. Sarina began talking with her two younger cousins, Nikhil and Mihir, and slowed down. Taking the hint, I boldly walked ahead with Neel.

"Now that the last year of school is almost over for you, are you excited about college?" he asked.

Can't he talk about anything other than studies? I thought.

"Not as much as I am about the summer."

"Oh, are you going to join the pool?"

"Probably not."

"Why?"

"Nimita is going to have a baby this summer. Since Mohini isn't here, Mummy will need help."

"I'll miss you," Neel said. His disappointment came through his low voice. "How is Mohini?"

"She's fine, I think . . ."

"Do you talk to her often?"

"Yes, my parents do," I said. My voice was thick and uneven.

"Maybe you can visit her sometime."

"Maybe."

"Come," he said, pulling my hand. Sarina, Nikhil, and Mihir followed us as we took off our sandals and walked to the edge of the water.

We buried our toes in the sand and listened to the waves.

We had left the heavy smell of sweet-and-sour chutney and spicy air behind. The sand was cool, and the breeze was as soft as a caress.

That night in bed, I played the walk over and over in my head until I'd memorized every single moment on the beach. If I studied like this for my exams I'd get excellent marks, I told myself.

A week later, when Sarina was visiting, Mummy told her, "I don't know what art you have, but you've certainly transformed Jeeta. Her tongue is not dipped in honey yet, but it isn't biting and hissing all the time. It satisfies me. It will serve her well."

"In her in-laws' house," I said under my breath, because I knew that's what Mummy meant. But of course she wouldn't say that to Sarina.

Sarina answered, "My family and I enjoy Jeeta as much as she enjoys us." Then she served a delicious slice of her smile.

From head to heart, Mummy was hers.

Of course I hadn't mentioned Neel to Mummy, but I wished I'd told Mohini about Neel before she left.

Once February ended and March had rolled to the middle, the sun was as bright and harsh as a shaved scalp. The heat was becoming unbearable now, and it was such a relief to go to Sarina's house and have an air-conditioned place in which to study. Around six in the evening the breeze from the ocean would begin to blow, and it felt wonderfully cool on the veranda.

It was the height of the green mango season, and Mummy made sour-and-hot mango pickles with a paste of mustard, fenugreek, and Kashmiri red peppers: and sweet mango pickles with sugar, ground cumin, and cinnamon sticks. I tasted the hot ones as if they were dabs of the fiery sun, and tasted the sweet ones as if they were rivers of honey with the logs of cinnamon floating away. After dinner I sucked on the cinnamon sticks that had simmered in the pickles. They were milder and softer.

The following weekend Mummy sent two jars of pickles with me to Sarina's house.

As exams got nearer Neel came over more and more. He had a unique way of learning. He studied something, then closed his books, shut his eyes, and sat like a statue. When I asked him what he was doing, he replied, "After I finish, I have to think about what I've read."

"Why?"

"It helps me digest it."

"What happens if you don't?"

"My brain gets stuffed up."

The closer it got to exam time, the less he studied.

The more time I spent with him, the more I wondered if he thought of me as a sister. All the things he did with Sarina he did with me: sat by me, touched me, looked at me and laughed with me, and teased me. After the walk on the beach, Sarina never asked me if I liked Neel, but just talked to me about him as if we'd both known him forever. Was she trying to tell me that Neel and I were just friends? I was afraid to ask.

One day while Sarina and I were studying Gujarati, we came across a figure of speech that we didn't understand. "Neel, do you know what this means?" Sarina asked.

Neel read it, closed his eyes for a few seconds, and explained, "It says, 'Your hair is like a rain cloud but a rain cloud has not your hair's softness.'"

"So, is the hair like a rain cloud or isn't it?" I asked.

"Not only is the hair as dark as a rain cloud, but it's more beautiful because it's softer."

"Is it a simile?" Sarina asked.

"Not a simple one. Because the hair is softer than a rain cloud, it's better than a rain cloud."

"There's a comparison and then there isn't. I'm confused," I said.

"I am too," Sarina said.

"Suppose I say that Jeeta's eyes are as bright as marigold blossoms. What is that?"

"A simile," we both said.

"But if I say, 'Jeeta's eyes are as bright as marigold

blossoms, but marigold blossoms can't speak like Jeeta's eyes can,' then I'm saying that not only are Jeeta's eyes as bright as marigold blossoms, but they're even more beautiful because they have the power to communicate."

By the time he'd finished speaking my ears were ablaze and my heart was his. Without looking at him I said, "I understand what you're saying, but how can anyone know what a rain cloud feels like?"

"Obviously the poet knows," Sarina said.

"He's saying that just to make someone feel special," I said doubtfully.

"What's wrong with that?" Sarina asked.

"It's wrong because he doesn't actually know if the rain cloud is softer than her hair," I babbled. "Not only has he never touched a rain cloud, but he probably has never touched her hair."

Neel and Sarina exchanged a glance.

"Sometimes one doesn't need to touch to feel," Neel said.

"If you can't touch hair, how can you tell if it's soft or coarse?"

"You can feel it with your heart."

"Feel hair with your heart!" Sarina said. "Neel, now you're a poet riding on a fine horse of imagination."

"If I had someone with hair softer than a rain cloud, I could fly on a horse of imagination."

"And don't forget the eyes, Neel. Eyes as bright as marigold blossoms but even more beautiful because they can speak."

"It's not that easy being a poet," I said, keeping my gaze fixed on my book. I wanted to prevent my eyes from speaking to him.

"It's the power of a special heart that can make me a poet," Neel whispered.

I looked at Sarina, but she'd hidden her face in her book.

Neel got up from his chair, saying, "Right now, the power belongs to our final exams, so let's not worry about soft hair and flying off on a horse of imagination. Study." He walked away from us, but not before stroking my hair.

It was impossible for me to concentrate after that. That night, while I was brushing my hair, I replayed the conversation in my head, trying to understand what Neel was saying. Had my eyes communicated what my heart felt? I wasn't sure. One thing was sure. Neel had power over my heart.

Two days later I waited thirty minutes to catch a bus to go to Sarina's house because one of the buses had broken down and the others were running full. I stood all the way through the ride and almost missed my stop because the bus was so crowded and I had to elbow people to get off. When I reached Sarina's house my head was pounding. Neel was there, and as soon as he saw me he asked, "What's wrong?"

"Nothing, just a headache from waiting in the heat."

"I could've picked you up."

I knew Mummy wouldn't allow that, but I couldn't say so to Neel. "It's okay. My house isn't on your way."

"I don't mind. Next time I'll pick you up."

"We'll worry about next time when next time comes," Sarina said. She knew that I couldn't ride with Neel, not by myself.

With the tips of her fingers, Sarina massaged my temples until my headache melted away.

Neel never asked about picking me up again, and I was relieved that he'd forgotten about it. It was so unlike him to forget, but he had, or at least I thought he had.

During the exams Mummy insisted that I stay at home. The entire exam week was hot, sleepless, and exhausting. Each day I had two three-hour exams. The fans whirled above me frantically while I wrote answers as fast as I could. In between exams I had an hour break for lunch, but I was too nervous to eat.

When I got home all I wanted to do was to take a bath, eat, and go to bed. But for the past month there had been a shortage of water, and we were getting water only for one hour in the morning, so there wasn't enough to take a bath in the evening. I would wash my face, hands, and feet, and drink a glass of cold buttermilk with roasted ground cumin and a little salt. Then I would fall asleep as I tried to study for the next day's exams, and have nightmares about them.

For the whole week I avoided the *Times of India* and the *Janmabhoomi Pravasi.* At exam time they always had reports of students throwing themselves in front of fast-coming trains or jumping off rooftops. Finally the exams were over. I had been so used to going to Sarina's house to study, it felt strange to spend an entire weekend at home.

We continued to follow the same routine on Sundays with Girishji and Nimita coming over for a big lunch. Now that my exams were over, I helped Mummy with the cooking. The kitchen was as hot as coal-burning *sagdi*, and I felt like I was a cob of corn getting roasted. As the perspiration plastered my blouse onto my back, I wondered why I'd bothered to take a bath that morning.

Nimita was very pregnant, very round, and very happy. Her stomach protruded below her blouse. Instead of wearing the light georgette and chiffon that she usually wore in summer, she wore heavier cotton saris. It helped, but did not completely hide her stomach. She ate a lot, too. Now Mummy fussed over both Girishji *and* Nimita.

Nimita moved slowly and clumsily. Every time she asked for something, Girishji would spring like a windup toy. Nimita said that in the morning when the smell of dal and spices made her sick to her stomach, Girishji would cook for her.

While Mummy and I cooked, Nimita and Girishji played cards or *carrom* with Chiraj and Vivek. I could hear their laughter and it made me happy. Sometimes, when Nimita was feeling fine, she would come and sit in the kitchen with us, and Girishji would talk to Pappa or teach Chiraj and Vivek how to play chess. I wished Mohini were there, too.

Nimita had a glow that Mummy said came from carrying a new life, but I felt it was also from Girishji's attention and love. I realized how much I liked Girishji now.

On Sunday afternoons, instead of embroidering, Mummy would ask me to read the *Bhagavad Gita*. She wanted the baby to hear good words and for Nimita to think pleasant thoughts. That way the soul that came would be a good soul. I wondered what kind of naughty thoughts Mummy had had when she was carrying me.

Foi had mentioned that Girishji was fond of *bhajans*, devotional songs, and sang beautifully. While growing up in the Sheth Tejpal Orphanage, he had led both the morning and evening prayers, but I'd never heard him sing. One afternoon Girishji sang for us. His voice was like mango juice—sweet, golden, and satisfying. When he finished, "*Ek ja de chingari, Mahanal,* Give me one light, the Great One," none of us could utter a word.

Finally I stole the silence. "What are you going to name your baby?"

"It depends on Baby's moon sign," he replied.

"Can't you figure that out now from the due date?"

"The moon sign changes every two to three days, so until the baby is born we won't know for sure. Most likely it will be *Vrushchik*, Scorpio, so the name will have to begin with an *N*, *Y*, or *U*. Can you think of any names?"

Neel came to my mind right away, but I didn't say so.

"There are so many names starting with N. How about Nimesh, Nainesh, Neelesh, Nayan, if it's a boy? If it's a girl, name her Nani Nimita, Little Nimita, to match her Mummy's name," I suggested.

"Anything but Nani Nimita. One of me is enough."

"Just joking. I'll make a list of both boys' and girls' names for you."

"Just boys' names, because they're sure to have a son," Mummy said.

Girishji was offended by Mummy's words. I could see it in his eyes. Nimita just shook her head.

"Why not names of both boys and girls?" I asked aloud, trying not to let my anger show.

Mummy made a sweeping motion and said, "Daughters and sons are as far apart as the earth and the sky. You give birth to both of them, nurse them, feed them, educate them, and then what? For a daughter you worry until you find her a suitable husband and get her married. A daughter keeps taking from you, and you're never done with your obligations. But a son is a different matter. *Deekro, jivta pale ane muva bale*, a son takes care of you while you're alive and cremates you when you die. When he gets married, the wedding doesn't sink you into debt, and his good wife takes care of all your needs. And when he performs the last rites, your soul rests in peace. A son is like having insurance for this life and the next, and who'd want to be without that?"

"That's not always true," I said.

"Ever since you've become friends with Sarina you think you're just like her. If a crow flies with a swan, that doesn't make the crow a swan. She's an only daughter, you remember that," Mummy said. "These days, an only girl is as good as a boy. She inherits everything, and some parents even let her perform the last rites, so it makes no difference. The laws have changed now, but in olden times if one didn't have a son, the inheritance went to nephews or cousins."

Was I a crow flying with a swan? And what if I were? There is nothing wrong with that as long as the crow and the swan are friends and want to be together. I thought about asking Mummy, May I go to the swan's house? But it wasn't the best way or the right time to ask. At three-thirty I volunteered to make tea, and that pleased Mummy.

While I was making tea, I thought about Mohini. How I missed her on Sundays. I wished she'd married someone like Girishji and could come home every Sunday. After everyone had sipped and slurped their tea from cup and saucer, I asked Mummy if I could go to Sarina's house.

"Go, if you want to, but be back by nine."

"I will," I said, singing inside, Yes, yes, yes, five hours to spend with Sarina!

When I got to Sarina's house she was taking a shower. There was no one there except Neel. "So how did the last exam go?" he asked as we sat on the balcony off the living room.

"The last one was the best."

"Was it history?" he said, bringing his chair closer to me.

"Yes. How did you know?"

"How could I not know?"

"What do you mean?"

"We've been studying in the same house for the past month. I'd have to be really *gamaar*, dull, not to notice what you enjoy and what you don't."

"Are you saying you're not *gamaar*?"

Neel bent toward me and, half whispering, said, "What do you think?"

"Does it matter?"

"If it didn't matter, why would I ask you?" He sat back in his chair and pierced me with his steady gaze.

My heart pounded, *dhamak dhum, dhum, dhamak, dhum*, getting louder by each beat. I focused my attention on a palm frond rocking back and forth. "Because you want me to say, 'Neel, you're not *gamaar*, you're brilliant.' "

He didn't answer. When I looked at him he held my gaze and wouldn't let it go. I felt my earlobes turning red. My whole face felt warm. What were we talking about? What did he want me to do? Or say? What did I want to say? What should I do? Why did Sarina have to take a shower now and leave me alone with him? My mind jumped from one thought to another.

He took my hand in his and asked, "When will I see you again?"

I wasn't ready for his question.

"I don't know."

"Next week?"

"I can't tell."

"Make it soon," he said.

He lifted my hand and kissed it.

fourteen

THE NEXT DAY Mummy asked me to help her make *ladu* for Nimita. These were not the usual sweet dessert *ladu* made with flour, sugar, and ghee. Besides flour and ghee, these contained brown sugar; ground fenugreek seeds that were so bitter, just the thought of them curled up my tongue; pungent powdered ginger; and ten other spices. I remembered Mummy making them while we were busy with our exams and giving Nimita a large stainless steel container full of them.

"Has Nimita been eating more than one *ladu* a day? Has she finished all the ones you gave her a few weeks ago?" I asked.

"These are different. These are to eat after the delivery, because they have something special in them. It will help Nimita not have back pain after the delivery," she said, pointing to a stone mortar and pestle containing *gunder*, the white semitransparent chunks secreted by the acacia tree.

I pounded the *gunder* while Mummy cooked the whole-wheat flour in ghee. It smelled delicious.

Then she opened up a jar of powdered ginger. It was so fine that some of it floated into the air and tickled my nose. I felt a sneeze coming on and turned away just in time to cover my nose with a handkerchief.

Everyone believed that one sneeze brought bad luck and two turned ill luck around. I knew making these *ladu* was important to Mummy, and she didn't want anything to go wrong with Nimita or the baby, so I was hoping for another sneeze, but it never came.

"What an ill time to sneeze!" Mummy said.

"I was planning on two sneezes."

"Show your teeth and wag your tongue as much as you want. Soon enough, the day will come when you'll wish you'd listened to me. If you keep your ego in front of your eyes and ears, someday you'll cry like a monsoon sky."

I didn't answer. After all, that's what she wanted.

We both took a handful of mixture in our hands and pressed it between our palms. She'd added extra ghee to it, and the mixture made a nice, round *ladu*, which she rolled in fine, brownish-white poppy seeds before setting them on a *thali*.

"Jeeta, in our time girls married whoever their parents said to marry and made the marriage work. I met your Pappa only once before our marriage. When I left my small town of Sihor and came to the big city of Mumbai, I didn't complain. Overnight, more than my name was changed. Overnight, I left more than my parents, uncle and aunt, and all my brothers and sisters: I left our big rambling house with the lush mango grove surrounded by thick *mehndi* hedges, the peacocks that came every morning to feed, the young Bharvad boys in bright clothes leading their cows and water buffaloes to the pasture land, the afternoon snack of freshly dug peanuts and brown sugar, the sound of temple bells ringing in the evening just as the dust from the returning cows' hooves covered the sky . . . but I didn't complain."

"Yes, Mummy."

"We believed in making the best of what befell us. Our parents and elders were older and wiser than us, and we respected them and the choices they made for us. In this new time, girls go out with boys five times and still say no to them. They keep their engagement for two years, get married, and then they change their minds. I ask, are they happier? I don't think so. I scold you for your own good. Keep your wandering mind under control and the rest will follow."

Her tone was wistfully gentle. She'd never talked to me with such power. It rattled me.

I thought about how brave Mummy was to move from a place like Sihor to Mumbai! That was a long, long time ago, and yet her voice revealed that she still missed those things. I wondered if Pappa was ever aware of what Mummy had left behind when she got married. Did he ever talk to her about her past and all the things that made her childhood? Did he ever try to understand her?

I helped Mummy clean up our bedroom from corner to corner. It was considered bad luck to get any of the baby's things ready until after the birth. But we could prepare all the things Nimita would need after the delivery. Mommy made a mixture of roasted sesame, fennel, and dill seeds, with dried, roasted coconut for Nimita to eat after dinner every day so that she'd have enough milk for nursing and the baby wouldn't get cramps. Chiraj, Vivek, and I liked the mixture so much that Mummy had to make twice as much as she'd planned.

The following Thursday, Nimita gave birth to a healthy

baby girl. Nimita's face glowed bright, and even in her dim eyes I could see sparkles.

When he picked the baby up for the first time, Girishji gleamed as though he were surrounded by a thousand lamps. She stared at him with her bright eyes and studied his face. He drew her close to his chest.

Hema Auntie came to see the baby. She looked at the baby as if she were an inspector in charge of giving out health certificates to newborns. "Well, at least the baby is healthy."

I was furious. Why did she have to say "at least"?

"Too bad you have three sons and no daughters; you'll never know what joy a daughter can bring to your life," I said.

Hema Auntie glared at me. She opened her mouth as if to speak, but her anger wouldn't let her. Instead she left in a huff, not waiting for Mummy to come.

"Why do you use such sharp words?" Nimita pleaded. "Please, for my sake, keep quiet."

"How can I keep quiet? Doesn't she annoy you?"

"I'm too happy to worry about what she or anyone else says. Aren't I?" she cooed to the baby.

"You're right. It doesn't matter. I won't say anything more."

One visitor commented, "With Nimita's eye problems, a boy would have been better, but in today's world we must believe both are the same." And another said, "The first one can be of any sex. Just hope the second one will be a boy to carry on Girishji's name."

Nimita's heart had no place to take in those words.

On my way back from the hospital, I bought two tiny, widemouthed clay pots for Mummy. When I got home Mummy filled one of the pots with castor oil and dipped a cotton wick in it. While it burned she partially covered it with the other clay pot. Black soot collected on the top of the second pot. Later, when the flame went out Mummy added a little ghee to the soot, mixing it together with her clean fingers until it turned into a smooth paste.

She placed the mixture in two small, round, silver boxes with a single rose engraved on each. This was the new kohl for the baby's delicate eyes.

"Here, you can have this one," she said, handing me one box.

I applied the jet-black kohl to my eyes. "I don't think I've ever used such soft and smooth kohl before."

"When you were a baby I did. Your eyes, they shone like onyx," Mummy said, giving me a kiss on the forehead.

I buried my head in the folds of her sari.

* * *

With the baby's arrival, Nimita's world quietly slipped into a new season. I was happy for her. It was still a few more days before the baby's naming ceremony, so we just called her "Baby." Nimita and Baby moved from the hospital to our house. Mummy had wanted Nimita to stay with us a month before Baby was due, but because Girishji was alone, Nimita didn't want to come. As much as I missed having my sisters around, I was glad that Nimita hadn't moved in with us earlier.

There was so much work and so little space with Baby and Nimita around. At six o'clock every morning, Gangabai, a massage lady, came for Nimita and Baby, and stayed for an hour. Gangabai was a tall, solidly built woman, with hands the size of banyan leaves. She would take her battered sandals off outside before entering the house.

Gangabai carried herself with a straight back and neck, with one end of her sari covering her head, and planted each step on the floor firmly but softly without making any noise. In the middle of her slightly raised, wide forehead she wore a red *bindi* as large as a betel nut. Gangabai wrapped her sari differently from us. She passed one end between her legs and tucked it in the back, creating a pair of pants. It gave her much more freedom to move around than the traditional Gujarati way of wrapping a sari around both legs together. As soon as she entered the apartment, she would head for the bedroom.

While Baby slept, Gangabai would give Nimita a massage. They spoke in low tones and I wondered what they were discussing. Then Nimita and Mummy would take their baths while Gangabai took care of Baby.

The first day I watched Gangabai, closely. Slipping her palm behind Baby's neck, she picked Baby up with one hand. Her index finger supported Baby's head and her big palm supported Baby's shoulders and back, while Baby's buttocks and feet dangled down. Sitting on the floor, she crossed her muscular legs at the ankles, undressed Baby, and laid Baby on her legs, facing up. Baby stared at Gangabai while Gangabai massaged her with almond oil and spoke to her in Marathi. As Gangabai talked, her large nose ring shifted back and forth, adding a language of its own. Once in a while she would try to speak in Gujarati. It was hilarious but I was afraid to laugh.

After the massage, Gangabai lifted Baby's arms and legs and moved them in a circle, crossed them, uncrossed them, flexed, and extended them. I was afraid that she might hurt Baby.

I told Mummy, "You'd better watch Gangabai. She handles Baby like a rag doll."

"I am not worried."

"You don't know what she does. While you're taking a bath she twists and turns her arms and legs."

"She did that to you too and you are in one piece," Mummy said.

"She did?"

"Yes, all of you. From Nimita to Vivek, she gave you all your massages and baths for the first six months of your lives, and she probably knows more about how to handle a new mother and a baby than a gynecologist or a pediatrician."

I wasn't so sure, but Baby didn't cry, and looked relaxed. After massaging Baby, Gangabai would put her down on a quilt by the window, where the morning sun rays were streaming in, before giving her a bath.

After Baby's bath I wanted to hold her and drink in all the softness and eat up all her sweet smell, but Nimita got Baby. I still couldn't take a bath because, while Nimita nursed Baby, Gangabai washed Nimita's and Baby's clothes in the bathroom. Before leaving, Gangabai would wrap Baby in a blanket and put her back in the cradle. Baby would sleep for three hours after that.

By the time Gangabai left, Pappa would be ready for his bath and I'd have to wait until he was done.

One day, before leaving, Gangabai said to Nimita, "Remember to do the exercises I showed you at least three times a day. It's important for your marriage."

"I'll do them," Nimita said.

"What exercises?" I asked as soon as Gangabai went out the door.

"After-delivery exercises."

"She said it would help your marriage. What did she mean by that?"

"When you have a baby your body changes. Things get all stretched out. These exercises help everything get back to their original size." She stopped, stared at me for a second, and continued. "Do you know what I mean?"

"Of course I do."

"It's important for our pleasure."

I didn't know what to say, and picked up my towel and clothes for my bath.

While taking my bath I thought of the time when Girishji didn't let Nimita come watch the movie with us. He was strict, demanding, and unreasonable. At that time Nimita was timid and afraid. All had changed now. Now they both seemed to want to please each other. After their marriage they had slowly and steadily fallen in love. I wondered if Mohini and Anoop were falling in love, too.

Girishji came every evening and ate dinner with us. Having extra people around made me want to run to a cave deep in the mountains. At night, when Nimita got up to feed Baby, I woke up too. Chiraj and Vivek had moved into the living room with Pappa, and both of them slept through the night like Himalayan bears.

But worst of all was the amount of work I had to do. The unending caravan of visitors that came to play with Baby only added to my work, because I had to serve them tea and snacks. I had no time to go to Sarina's house and no excuse to see Neel. I missed him so much, one day I asked Mummy if I could go to the Hanging Gardens.

"With your pappa?"

"No."

"Then who? Sarina?" Before I could answer her she added, "Call her. If she's free, you can go."

"I will."

Mummy stood there waiting for me to call.

I had no choice but to dial the number. Sarina picked up the phone.

"This is Jeeta," I said. "Would you like to go to the Hanging Gardens this evening?"

"What?"

"I'll meet you at six by the front gate, and if you can bring . . ."

"Neel?"

"Yes," I said, and hung up.

Mummy shook her head. "That was the shortest conversation I have ever heard on the phone. Even when people call us by mistake they talk longer than this."

"We will talk in person. It is better that way."

That evening I applied the fresh kohl Mummy had made. I trembled at the thought of Mummy finding out I was meeting Neel.

When I got to the Hanging Gardens, Neel and Sarina were not there. I strolled near the gate, but felt awkward pacing alone. What if she didn't hear the time right? Surely, she would ask Neel to come. But what if she didn't?

I sat on a bench and watched three black ants carry a piece of puffed rice. It kept falling, and they kept lifting it up. They were determined to take it home. I was so engrossed watching them, I didn't see Neel coming until he said, "I didn't know studying ants was your hobby. May I watch them with you?"

"You're late."

"I didn't say I would be here at six."

"That's true. Where is Sarina?"

"She couldn't come. What was that strange phone call about? She told me you were in a hurry, as if you only had a minute to live. What happened?" he asked as he sat close to me and put his arm around me.

"I missed you. I had to see you."

"Go on."

"That's it."

We strolled all around the park. He listened while I told him about all the work I had to do at home and how good it felt to be with him. Then he walked me to a spot from where we could watch the sunset. We stood quietly holding hands. I remembered Yamini saying how holding hands wasn't romantic. How wrong she was!

On the eleventh day we had the naming ceremony for Baby. Girishji and Nimita had picked out a name and had told Foi what it was. Usually the father's sister would name the baby during the naming ceremony, but because Girishji didn't have any relatives, Foi did it.

The ceremony was on a Sunday, and Mummy, Foi, and I prepared lunch for about fifty relatives. Besides dal, rice, fried whole-wheat *puris*, tomato chutney, shredded carrots, and sesame salad, hot cayenne pepper pickled in lemon juice and turmeric, we made hors d'oeuvres of *khandvi*: thin rolls of buttermilk and chickpea flour with spices. For dessert, we served *rassgulla*, creamy white balls of cheese in light syrup.

The naming ceremony took only half an hour. We said a prayer to Lord Ganesha first, and then Foi wrapped Baby in soft cotton. Mummy spread the silk blanket on the floor. Chiraj and Vivek each held one corner, and I held two corners on the other side, turning the cloth into a cradle. Foi laid Baby in it, and we gently swung her, singing:

> *"Oli Zoli pipal pann,*
> *Foi'a padyu 'Nupur' nam.*
> *(Baby) swings on the leaf of a pipul tree*
> *Foi gives her a name, Nupur."*

Mummy gave Foi a coconut, a silk sari, and a pair of gold bracelets for naming Nupur. It was nice to finally have a name for her. I was so tired of saying Baby this and Baby that, I decided that I'd name my children on the day they were born.

The lunch lasted a couple of hours, and by night I was

worn out. Even though Nupur got gifts of six silver rattles, three silver cups, a silver plate and bowl set, and some cotton dresses with embroidery, she wasn't pleased. That night she cried and cried. I thought it was from seeing so many people, but she continued to wake up and cry until two in the morning every night. Nimita slept in the morning while Nupur took a nap, but I couldn't. I was exhausted.

When Nupur was twenty days old, Nimita went back to her house. Mummy wanted her to stay longer, but Girishji insisted they come home. As they walked down the steps, Girishji carried Nupur in one arm and kept one arm around Nimita. He was proud, happy, excited, and all his emotions were rolled into one grin that filled half of his face. I wondered how many sleepless nights it would take before his grin was replaced by a red-eyed, worn-out look.

After Nupur and Nimita left, Mummy said she didn't like being in an empty house. She started going to temple twice a day and told me all the things she wanted me do while she was out. I was willing to help her, until I realized that she'd dumped all the cooking on me.

Our servant, Naran, did the dishes, laundry, and cleaned the house, but we had no cook. For breakfast I served leftover *rotli* with milk, which was easy.

Lunch was a big headache, though. Soon after my bath, I cut the vegetables and cooked them, adding ginger, red pepper, turmeric, cumin, and coriander. I washed the lentils and rice and put them in the pressure cooker, and then made dough for the *rotli*. After the lentils were cooked, I added spices and let them simmer for a while. I rolled the *rotli* and cooked it on the stove.

As I rolled the *rotli* I thought of Mohini. It was difficult to roll and cook without her. It was strange to work silently for two hours. It was impossible to stop missing her.

One day I made tomato, cucumber, and onion salad with yogurt and dill, Mohini's favorite. I tried a spoonful but choked with sadness. I never made it again.

Every day around three o'clock Chiraj and Vivek were hungry. I had to make a snack for them and then in the evening I had to make dinner. Without Mohini, the kitchen had turned into a jail.

Pappa brought baskets full of mangoes, but they didn't cheer me up. They only added to my work. Every two or three days I picked out ripe mangoes nestled in the straw from the basket, then washed them and made them soft with my fingers while rotating them in my hand. I squeezed the pulp out and strained it through a fine wire mesh. Unlike orange juice, the mango goop sat on the wire mesh till I rubbed it and nudged it again and again. When I was done, my hands were so sore that I never wanted to see another mango in my life.

I washed all the mango pits a few times and then took them up on the terrace to dry on an old cotton sari. After a couple of days, Chiraj broke the pits open and we boiled the soft, beige *gotli* that was inside, and sucked on it after our meal. Even though it tasted delicious, just like mangoes, I never wanted to see another *gotli* in my life. It had only been a couple of months since Mohini had left, but it felt like years had gone by.

Mohini called every Sunday. When I was at Sarina's house I'd missed her phone calls, but for the last few Sundays I'd talked to her. There was something wrong with being connected by two mouthpieces and receivers. I longed to touch Mohini's long fingers, see the curls on her forehead, feel her warm breath next to me. I couldn't forget that we were miles of ocean and land apart.

And I missed her more after hearing her voice. I played our conversations over and over again, trying to find out if she was happy, if Anoop was good to her, if all was well in her world.

Mohini told me she liked Naperville, Illinois. It was very close to Chicago. She'd been to Chicago a few times and said that it was a clean and beautiful city with tall buildings and a lake that was so big it had waves. I tried to picture a lake as big as an ocean, but couldn't.

I wasn't sure how happy Mohini was. For one thing, she never mentioned meeting new people or any friends of Anoop's. She'd found a job in a bank, so I knew that throughout the week she was busy, but I wondered what they did on Saturdays and Sundays. Once when I asked her about friends, she said cheerfully, "Oh, we've been so busy that we haven't had any time." I tried to believe her.

One day after Mohini's call, Mummy said, "Mohini seems happy in her new surroundings and probably doesn't miss us as much. I think as soon as she gets used to her new home, she probably won't call us every week."

"It's not like she calls us every day. We need to talk to her once a week," I said.

"It costs a lot. She can write us letters."

"If she can't call, I will. I'll pay the bill with my money."

"Listen to the one with a big purse and a big mouth."

"Why are you two arguing?" Pappa said. "We'll worry about calling Mohini if and when she stops calling us."

That afternoon when I was done cooking lunch, the heat made me sick. I had not seen Neel since our evening in the Hanging Gardens. I had talked to Sarina on the phone a few times, but it wasn't enough. In my frustration, I tore a piece of paper from my notebook and wrote to Chiraj and Vivek:

> I will cook only twice a day. For the rest of the day the two of you can cook, beg, or buy your food. You can get it from the cabinet, stores, or restaurants. I don't have ten hands, so why should I have to do all the work? My ears are filled with the words, "I'm hungry. What can I eat? We had that two days ago. What are our other choices? I want more. I'm still hungry!" This happens every day—actually more than once a day. You know what food we eat and where it is just as well as I do, so why do you ask me? Why do I have to give you all the choices? Make a list of the food you want, and do whatever you have to do to fix it: wash it, peel it, cut it, mix it, cook it. Maybe offer me a bite and . . .

I couldn't write any more.

I wanted to tape the note next to the stainless steel water dipper. That way when they went to get a drink of water from the red earthen pot, they'd see it. But I was afraid that if Mummy read my note she'd get mad. So I tore it into tiny pieces and threw it out the window and watched it float to the ground. Waiting for Mummy to leave for temple, I fell asleep on the couch. Vivek came and nudged my arm. "Wake up, Jeeta. Mummy's been gone for an hour and I'm hungry. What can I eat?"

"Eat a pigeon," I said, bolting upright. I stared at him until tears rolled down my cheeks.

Vivek ran to Chiraj. Chiraj went in the kitchen and brought a glass of water, handed it to me, and then began to gently rub my back. Vivek sat on the floor fanning me with a peacock feather fan, tightly clutching its bamboo handle.

"Why are you crying, Jeeta?" Vivek kept asking me. He squinted his eyes, searching my face.

I grabbed him and pulled him close to me.

"It's fine if you don't talk. You'll live longer," he said.

"What?"

"Mr. Shah told our class that everyone gets a set number of words in life to use. When that number is used up, you die."

I smiled.

"Mr. Shah tells the same story to his class every year. He told us the same thing," Chiraj said, shaking his head. "He wants you to be quiet, that's all."

Vivek looked confused. I told him, "Mummy, Foi, and

Hema Auntie all talk much more than Pappa or Fua. Don't you think that for every word given to men, ten words are given to women?"

"At least," Chiraj said.

We all laughed.

Chiraj went back into the kitchen. A few minutes later he came out with a mixture of fried yellow lentil mixed with pomegranate, chopped onions, and raw mango pieces, and three spoons. He surprised me; I didn't think he even knew how to cut a pomegranate or chop an onion so finely. The three of us ate from the same bowl.

I called Sarina and talked to her for a while.

"Come over tomorrow and spend a day with me, and I'll change your mood," she said.

After dinner I asked Mummy if I could go to Sarina's house.

"What will I do without you?"

"For one day can't you do without me? I work so hard every day. Even Naran gets a day off every week, and you won't let me spend a day with my friend. I'm going!"

"*Choop*. If you ever talk like that again I'll pull your tongue out. I wasn't much older than you when I had a home, a husband, and a child on the way. And I was grateful."

It was futile to say a word. I took out one of Mohini's novels and flipped through the pages.

Five minutes later Mummy came and took my hands in hers. "You can go to Sarina's house tomorrow, but be back around five."

I was surprised Mummy gave me permission after I had talked back to her. Did she realize how much work I was doing these days, and feel guilty? Or did she remember how it was when she was my age, and want me to be happy? No matter what the reason, I was glad Mummy had changed her mind.

fifteen

IN THE MORNING I helped Mummy before I went to Sarina's house. When I left at ten, the heat bit and pinched my neck and my back. Sarina poured me a tall glass of green mango drink, and we sat on her bed.

I touched the icy glass to my cheeks and let the heat evaporate.

"I'm glad you came today, because we're leaving for Mount Abu tomorrow," Sarina said.

Mount Abu was not too far from Nathdwara, where we'd gone for the haircutting ceremony for Chiraj and Vivek.

"That'll be fun," I said, wishing that I could get out of burning Mumbai.

"Neel wants to know if you can meet him the day after tomorrow."

"Unless the sky collapses, there's no chance I can convince Mummy."

"Try."

"Why isn't he here?" I said. I had been hoping Neel would come around noon and stay until five.

"He's not coming."

I was so disappointed, I didn't want Sarina to see my face. I took a big sip of my drink and kept my face covered with my glass. I kept on drinking until I'd finished the sour green mango juice sweetened with brown sugar.

"Why not?" I said when I was done.

"Ask him when you see him."

Sarina had promised to change my mood. So far she hadn't helped. Both of us sat quietly and avoided looking at each other.

Finally she spoke. "I'm tired of being a messenger. It'd be nice if you and Neel would discuss your own plans."

"I would, but Mummy—"

"That doesn't mean I have to answer to both of you, does it? I don't like being a go-between."

"You don't have to. I'll talk to Neel," I said. "Besides, you're leaving tomorrow, so you won't have to worry about us for a while."

Sarina looked as though she were fighting tears. I

realized how occupied I'd been with my own feelings. When I was with Neel it was as if the whole world slipped away. Sarina must feel lonely when she's with us, I thought. Sarina had been so good to me and I'd been too selfish to care.

"What will you do in Mount Abu for ten days?" I asked.

"Horseback riding, and walking."

"Maybe you'll meet someone interesting there."

"Maybe."

"You still haven't met Kiran yet. You should go to Yamini's house after you get back. Maybe I can go with you."

"Don't worry about setting me up."

"I wasn't. I can't imagine anyone doing that for you."

"What do you mean?"

"You'll never go for the traditional arranged marriage route."

"Why not? If someday I want to get married but haven't fallen in love, I would want Mummy and Pappa to arrange for me to meet someone."

"You would?" My voice came out squeaky with surprise. Was she kidding? It didn't sound like it.

"Nowadays, arranged marriages aren't like old times,

when you would meet just once and then decide. Isn't it nice to meet someone that your parents already know about? Isn't it good that they know the family well, too? Look at Nimita and Girishji. Aren't they happy?"

"Yes. I suppose."

As I stood in line for the bus, the wind picked up making the dust swirl. It hit my face and stung my eyes. I heard a deep, long, rumble that seemed to come out of the ocean's belly. Was it an echo of thunder? It couldn't be. It was still May, the month of dry heat, mango, and brown landscape. By the time the bus came my hair was spilling all over my face.

On the bus I thought about Sarina saying she wouldn't mind meeting someone her parents suggested. It had surprised me at first, but then I realized that Sarina was as open to an arranged marriage as she was to finding her own partner in life. The raindrops started plopping on the bus windows. I watched the vendors as they hurriedly gathered up their wares: edible gourds and bunches of coriander, palmistry books, brass statues of Lord Ganesh, Shiva, and Krishna.

By the time I got off the bus, it was raining hard. The monsoon was more than three weeks away and not a single person had an umbrella. I was drenched, soaked right to my bones when I got home.

That evening, when I answered the phone, Mohini was on the line. It was not Sunday morning and I was shocked to hear her voice.

"Why are you calling today?" I asked.

"I wanted to talk to you. Can't I call when I feel like talking?"

"How are you? You seem down."

"I'm fine," she said, and cleared her throat. "Just a little cough."

"Are you sick?"

"No. Maybe homesick."

"Oh, Mohini! I miss you so much."

"I miss all of you. I . . . I never realized how hard it is to be away from home."

"How is Anoop?"

"He's fine." Her voice was cold and even, as if Anoop were nothing but an acquaintance.

"Is he there?"

"No, he just left for work. I have to go now, too. I'm so glad I got to talk to you."

"But we really haven't said anything."

"Bye."

"Mohini . . . Mohini?"

There was no answer. I couldn't figure out why Mohini had called. Did she just want to hear my voice? Did she want to tell me something and then changed her mind? But what? Maybe I was taking her simple straight words and bending them in all different directions. Stop guessing, I told myself.

That night the thoughts I'd pushed away wiggled back. I fell asleep thinking about Mohini, and my sleep was filled with a caravan of dreams. In my dreams Mohini was with me. In the morning only her worries were with me.

Sarina was in Mount Abu and there was no one else I could talk to.

I came up with an excuse to see Neel the next day. "Mummy, I haven't played with Nupur for a few days. What if I go spend an afternoon with her tomorrow? Nimita would like that, wouldn't she?"

"Yes, she would."

I was so happy with myself, I couldn't stop humming. When Mummy went out, I called Neel. "Can you meet me by Crawford Market?"

"Yes, what time? Maybe we can have lunch together."

"I only have half an hour."

"That's all? It takes longer to get there."

"I know, but that's all I have. I'm supposed to be at Nimita's."

"I'll drop you near her house. It'll give us a little more time."

I hesitated for a second, then said, "Sure."

But in the evening, my humming, my good fortune, and my plans were all blown away. I felt chills up and down my back, and my hands and feet turned ice cold. It was hot and muggy out, but I couldn't stop shaking, and then sneezing.

"The ill-timed rain brings sickness as fast and furious as a wild horse," Mummy said. She made me hot milk with sugar and tapioca and rubbed my arms and legs to warm them up. My mouth tasted as if I'd eaten bitter neem, and my throat hurt.

"You're not going to see Nupur tomorrow. Nimita needs a sick guest as much as farmer needs a dead bullock."

I had no strength to answer Mummy. All I could do was close my eyes and hope I felt better in the morning.

The next day I left a message for Neel that I was sick and wouldn't be able to see him.

My sickness turned into pneumonia, and for the next week I lay in bed all day long and listened to Mummy jabber away like a talking parrot. Mummy repeated the stories she'd heard at temple. For the first time in my life, I realized that Mummy went to temple more for gossip than for God.

When Sarina came back from Mount Abu, she and Neel came to see me. They brought a green coconut and a bouquet of roses. When I saw Neel my heart jumped twice, the first time because he was there, the second time because I was afraid of what Mummy would say. If Mummy was upset or mad, she hid it very well, and was polite, especially when Sarina said Neel was her cousin.

The green coconut was from Sarina's courtyard. One end was shaved off into a cone shape. Sarina got a knife from the kitchen and Neel cut off the top of the cone and stuck a straw in it and handed it to me. With all the medication I was taking I was afraid that the coconut water would taste bitter, but it was sweet and flavorful. After I finished the water Neel took out a thin layer of coconut meat from the empty cavity with a knife and piled it on a small plate. Unlike the heavy, thick coconut meat from a brown coconut, this was soft and thin. It was a challenge to pick up the slippery pieces that slid away from my fingers when I tried to put them in my mouth.

We didn't talk much. With Mummy right there, we had to be careful about what we said, but it was fine. At least I was able to see them both.

"I hope you'll feel good enough to come and stay with

me in two weeks," Sarina said softly when Mummy went in the kitchen to get a snack for them.

"I don't think I can."

"By that time you'll feel fine," Neel said.

"You promised to stay with me when my parents go to Goa for the conference."

"I'll try," I said, remembering that I had told Sarina that I'd spend a weekend with her in late May. I'd asked Mummy a long time ago, too, but now I wasn't sure if I wanted to go. Just this short visit of theirs had made me tired.

I was afraid that Mummy would notice the way I looked at Neel, or the way he'd touched my hand before leaving, and scold me, but she didn't. One thing about Mummy was, unless she suspected something, she didn't notice much. I was grateful for that.

The second I saw Sarina Tuesday afternoon I knew something was terribly wrong. I sat up in my bed with two pillows behind me. When she brought the chair closer to me to sit down I saw that her face was all red. She sat down, put her book on the table, changed her mind, picked up her book, and put it on her lap. I looked at the cover and thought, she must be *pagel*, crazy, to carry her books now.

"Sarina, what would you like to drink?" Mummy asked.

"Tea would be nice. But only if you're making it for yourself."

Mummy and I both stared at her.

"Only two days ago I tried tea for the first time. I like it," Sarina said.

"Don't get into the habit of drinking it, though. Without my morning and afternoon cup of tea I feel as sluggish as a water buffalo in the summer heat. It's terrible," Mummy said, walking toward the kitchen.

As soon as Mummy had gone, Sarina took out a letter from her book and slipped it in my hand, whispering "Don't look at it now, just hide it."

I recognized the aerogramme. "Is it from Mohini?"

"Yes."

"Why did she send me a letter to your address?" I mumbled, my heart wildly beating *dhuk, dhuk, dhuk,* as I slipped the letter into the pillowcase.

I wanted to rush to the bathroom and read it, but my blouse and skirt had no pockets and I didn't want Mummy to discover my letter, not until I knew what was in it.

I closed my eyes while Mummy and Sarina drank their

tea. Even with my eyes closed I knew Mummy drank her tea from a saucer, like a cat licking milk from a bowl. Sarina sipped hers daintily from the teacup.

"You haven't finished even half a cup," Mummy said, getting up. "What's the problem? Don't you like my tea?"

"Oh yes, I like it very much, but it's very hot."

"I see," Mummy said, adding, "If you're planning to stay here for a while, I'll go to temple."

"Yes, yes, go ahead. I'll stay."

Sarina watched Mummy from the window as she went down the stairs, through the courtyard, and out of sight.

"Please read it," I said, handing Sarina the letter.

"Are you sure?"

"Yes."

She read:

Dear Jeeta,

You must be surprised to get this letter. Believe me, I wouldn't have written to you if I could have avoided it. When I first arrived here I missed all of you, but I was excited about starting a new life in a new land with Anoop. In the beginning it seemed that my dream was coming true. Anoop was very charming and funny. (Wasn't that the reason I decided to marry him so quickly?) Slowly, though, his temper began to flare. It didn't take much. I never told you this, but he slapped me once in Matheran and he's started doing the same here. If I set the table wrong (yes, there is a proper way to set a table) or didn't wear my hair down, he yelled, "How can I take you to meet my friends when you look and act so desi?"

Well, I am a desi and so is he, so what's wrong with acting like one?

The harder I tried, the less I seemed to please him. As time went by I realized that we never met anyone. I wondered if he had any friends. Hardly anyone called and he was rude with the neighbors, too.

One day when he came home from work, he saw me talking to Mr. Dobbs, who lives next door. Anoop lost his temper and slapped me hard across the face. Remember when Mummy used to occasionally slap us? We felt so little and powerless then. I felt the same way, only worse. I know you always had more courage than me to stand up to Mummy. How I wished I had that!

That night Anoop was apologetic and took me out to a fancy restaurant for dinner. With the right side of my face swollen and my eyes blood-shot from crying, I didn't want to go, but I was afraid to refuse. It seemed like he wanted the whole world to see what he'd done to me. The world that didn't know us and wouldn't dare to ask what had happened.

That night, as I lay on our bed crying, I decided to look for work. When Anoop found out that I wanted to work, he laughed. He said no one would hire me until I got rid of my heavy accent. About a week later, when my face was back to normal, I went to the bank in our neighborhood and luckily they hired me right away. Anoop was shocked.

My boss, Karen, is considerate and caring. It is like having part of you and Nimita here. Bosses and the people under them can talk much more freely here than in India. I felt awkward with my Indian accent, but slowly I opened up.

At home I told Anoop nothing of what went on at work. It was my private, unpolluted world. He thought all I did at the bank was work,

work, and work. As time went by he told me I couldn't call home because it was getting too expensive.

Two weeks ago he punched me again for putting his pants into the dryer by mistake. I hit the shelf of the kitchen cabinet above my right eye, and we had to rush to the hospital. When the doctor asked me what happened, I had to lie, for Anoop stood there holding my hand, looking very concerned. At that point I knew I hated him.

Don't worry about the wound. It's healing well. At work Karen asked me what had happened, and over lunch I told her the truth. She begged me to leave Anoop and said I could stay with her as long as I wanted to. I'm scared and confused. If I leave Anoop, what will happen to our family's reputation? And yet I can't stay. One day I'm afraid he'll really hurt me. Of all of us sisters and brothers, you have the most courage. Please tell me what I should do. Karen says I can file for a divorce. I don't know anyone in our family who's been divorced. Divorce here is not considered bad, and divorced women, even the ones with children, marry again. Often, even widows remarry. On one *hand that seems like the right solution, but will anyone want to marry a daughter from our family again?*

I know this letter is long and rambling. I haven't asked you how everyone is. I hope all of you are well.

Karen's address is on the back of this page. Write soon. If you can, call me in the morning after eight o'clock my time. Help me.

Your sister,
Mohini

By the time Sarina had finished the letter, we were both crying. Sarina got up and gave me a long hug. "We must do something fast," she said, wiping her eyes and folding the letter.

"Yes, we must," I said in a daze. "This can't be happening to Mohini. Only a few months ago she was with us, and now she's with this monster. . . . Why didn't Mohini tell me that Anoop hit her? I remember her looking lost and sad, but I thought it was because she was unhappy about leaving us. Why didn't I ask her? Why didn't I talk to Pappa about it? Then maybe I could've stopped her from going to America. I guess I was too busy with my own life. It's my fault, and now she's in danger and so far away! I don't know what I can do from here."

"Show the letter to your mummy."

"I can't."

"Why not?"

"Because that's exactly what Mohini doesn't want me to do. Otherwise she'd have written her a letter."

"When is your pappa coming back?"

"In a week."

"That's a long time. Do you want to talk to my parents?"

"No, Sarina. If I did that, Mummy and Pappa would never forgive me."

"You can't wait for a week."

"I know," I said, biting my lower lip. "I must help Mohini myself."

"How?"

"Can you come back around seven tonight and give me a ride?"

"What? Why?" Sarina said, lifting her eyebrows. "Your mummy wouldn't let you go out at night."

"Leave that up to me. I'll plead and beg until she lets me."

That evening, before Sarina came, I complained about getting bored and being cooped up in our apartment.

Mummy was happy to see me go for a ride. "Keep the windows rolled up," she said, tying a silk scarf around my throat.

"Take us a few blocks from here," I said to the driver, "and stop at the long-distance telephone stand." Whenever I saw those stands at every corner, I wondered who used them. Most people I knew had a telephone at home, or used their neighbor's, but today I was happy that public phones were available. I'd brought two hundred rupees in my pocket, my savings from my allowance.

My hands trembled as I dialed Mohini's telephone number. "Please, please let Mohini be alone," I mumbled.

"Hello," she answered.

"Mohini? It's me, Jeeta. Are you alone?"

"Yes, it is after eight o'clock in the morning here. He's gone to work."

"Listen, you must get out of that house, today."

"But . . . I . . ."

"You can't wait. Not for a second."

"Have you talked to anyone?"

"Are you worried about Mummy? She doesn't know anything at all. Pappa's in Jaipur and won't be back for another week. Give me Karen's number and I'll call you at her house in two days. Do it, because that's what I'd do if I were in your place."

Silence.

"Please, Mohini. You have to."

"Are you sure?"

"Absolutely."

"Then I will."

"Today?"

"Yes," she said with a firm voice. I let out my breath and hung up.

The next day, when Nimita came over with Nupur, I wanted to tell her about Mohini, but I never got a chance to be alone with her, even for a few minutes. She must have noticed something in my voice, because she asked, "What's wrong with you? All of a sudden you're not tired and sick anymore. Why are you so squirmy and agitated?"

"I'm feeling much better, and now I'm worried about my results. They will be out in two weeks."

"I suppose," she said, giving me a lingering look.

Mummy heard us, but didn't say a word. That made me feel better. The more I thought about what Mummy would do if she found out about Mohini and Anoop, the more convinced I was that she'd have a hard time believing that a nice man like Anoop from such a fine family could be violent. Or she might get hysterical and then the whole community would know and rumors would fly. They say you can't tie a sieve on people's mouths, and who knows what kind of garbage might come out.

Foi came to see me that afternoon. "It's great to see you walking around. Are you feeling better?" she asked.

"Much better," I said, trying to hide tears. After Pappa, she was the one who could solve a problem at our house, and seeing her made my courage melt in an instant. Just like Nimita, she gave me a lingering look and shook her head.

When Mummy wasn't there Foi asked me to come and sit by her. I knew she suspected something. "Are you getting your period normally?"

"Yes."

"There's a shadow on your face, a shadow darker than your dark skin. I can't ignore it. What's the matter, *beta*?" she said, rubbing my back softly.

I bit my lip. "Nothing."

I was shaking, but I knew I must keep it all inside me.

She held me tight. "As long as you can solve your problem, I don't want to interfere; yet you know that I'm always here for you."

"Thank you," I said, and I really, truly meant it.

Two days later, Sarina took me for a ride again. I called Karen's house, and Mohini was there. Her voice was shaky and I asked her what was wrong.

"I wrote a note to Anoop before I left."

"You didn't tell him where you were going, did you?"

"No, of course not. But he knows where I work, so he came to the bank and asked me to go out for lunch with him. He was polite, but when I refused to go with him, he threatened me. He started swearing in Gujarati, '*Salli, tara tukede-tukda kari fanki daish.*'" She began sobbing.

"*Bapre!* He wants to cut you in pieces and throw you out! Mohini, he's going to kill you if he gets a chance," I said. I paused for a breath. "Listen, do you have any money?"

"I have some, and I can borrow from Karen."

"Take the earliest flight and come home."

"What will happen to all of us . . . ? You . . ."

"Come home. You're much more important than any fake reputation. Call Sarina's house and leave a message with your flight number and when you'll be arriving. I'll be at the airport to meet you."

When I got back to the car I asked Sarina, "Is it all right if Mohini stays at your house with me?"

"Of course."

"Shouldn't we ask your parents?"

"No, Jeeta. If they know about it, then they'll have to worry about not telling your mummy. If they don't know, no one can blame them."

"But then you'll be in the middle."

She put her hand on my shoulder. "I'll be fine."

"It's only for two days, until Pappa comes home; I hope it works out."

"Quit worrying. My grandfather used to hide freedom fighters in his house for days when the whole British Raj was looking for them. I can certainly be brave enough to keep Mohini for two days."

On Saturday morning, I was edgier than a monkey. After lunch I got my bag ready and told Mummy that I was going to Sarina's house.

"Do you have to go? You're not completely cured."

"I promised her months ago."

That night Mohini and I were both tired: she from her long trip, and I from going to the airport to meet her. I didn't notice when we passed by the Haji Ali Dargah tomb and the Race Course. All I remember was holding Mohini's hand as we drove to Sarina's house. I wished we could've talked, but it was after two A.M. by the time we'd parked the car in Sarina's courtyard. Mohini took a shower, and then we went to bed.

After a long time I was able to sleep well, knowing that in the darkness I could hear her breathing and reach with my hand and touch her.

I came home the next morning, right before Pappa arrived. After he finished his tea, Mummy went to take her shower. That is when I told him what had happened. His face seemed to shrink and his lips trembled.

After a long silence, he asked, "How's Mohini?"

"She's lost some weight. Otherwise, I think she's fine."

"As soon as we get her home we'll take care of her weight."

"Will everything work out?"

"Absolutely. I'll make sure it does. You're my brave little tiger," he said, putting his hand on my head.

"What about Mummy?"

"You haven't said a word to her?"

"No. I wasn't sure how she'd react. I didn't want her to be upset."

"Yes, that's true," he said, looking out the window. A couple of pigeons were cooing and fluttering about. I don't think Pappa saw them. He was in his own shell of thoughts.

"You did the right thing," he said, taking a deep breath. "At present, let's tell everyone that Mohini missed us and is visiting us. I will tell Mummy the truth in a few days."

"Why not now?"

"I'm afraid when Mummy finds out what happened she will ask too many questions and make Mohini miserable. Let Mohini recover first."

When Mummy saw Mohini she rushed to give her a hug, saying, "It is good to have you back. Anoop is wonderful to send you home so soon!"

Mohini cringed as tears rolled out of her eyes. The next day Mummy made Mohini's favorite dishes.

sixteen

THE FOLLOWING MONDAY, our exam results were announced. On that day I woke up early and waited by the door for the newspaper. I grabbed the paper from the carrier and searched for my number in second class. It was not there. I looked in the third class and it was not there. I nearly collapsed. What if I'd failed? With trembling hands I flipped to the previous page, looked up, and saw that my number was in first class with a D next to it! I'd passed with distinction! I closed the newspaper, opened it again, and checked my number. It was still there. I had to believe it. As expected, Sarina passed with distinction, too. The phone rang and it was Sarina, happy and excited for both of us. As soon as I hung up, Neel called to congratulate me.

"Who was that?" Mummy asked.

"Sarina's cousin."

"Oh, to congratulate you, I suppose."

"Yes. Isn't it wonderful, Mummy? I can go to any college I want and study whatever I want to."

"Sure," she said. "If you get a Bachelor of Science, half of our problem is solved."

"I want to study law."

"*Ja, ja*, nonsense! Can you honestly see yourself arguing . . ." She stopped in midsentence. "I suppose you would make a good lawyer, but it won't do. A science degree is all you need. Law school is a long ladder that you'll never climb."

"Why won't I? I'm determined to become a lawyer."

"*Wah*, a lawyer! Have you looked at your face in the mirror? You have to look sharp, smart, and need many years of studying. It isn't for you. Like your sisters, if you're lucky, you'll be married in a few years. You're no *pundit*, scholar, you know."

"I may not be a *pundit*, but I want to be a lawyer."

"All this time I let you go to Sarina's house thinking you'd do well in your exams and then get a science degree. In these financially challenging times boys prefer an educated girl who can get a good-paying job and work for at least a few years. I'm giving you advice so that you'll have a bright future. If you go into science, the first boy you meet will say yes."

"I'm not studying for someone else. I want a career I can enjoy."

"Career, bareer—doesn't matter to me! You've always done whatever pleases you. At least once, listen to me. I'm only thinking about your future. All I want is to find a good family for you to be married into. These days all I hear is, 'Everything being equal, science graduates are preferred over any other graduates.' "

Even though I knew what she meant, I asked, "Preferred by whom?"

"By boys and their families."

"I want someone who wants to marry me for who I am, and not for my degree. If they only value a degree in science, then they should study and earn the degree themselves."

She stared at me and shook her head. "You can argue your way through a mountain."

"Exactly! I'll make a great lawyer."

"Get admission and you can always change your mind."

As soon as I got my transcripts I went to Jai Hind College and enrolled in their liberal arts program.

* * *

Mohini had gone to Nimita's house for couple of days. I wanted to go with her, but Nimita's house was filled with Nupur's stuff, and there wasn't enough room for Mohini and me both to be there at the same time.

How I wished Mohini were home so we could go up on the terrace and talk. I thought if Pappa were in town I could've talked to him, but lately he was never there when I needed him. It was Mummy who was there, and I wished Mummy and I could understand each other better. Later in the morning, when I went out to buy vegetables, Chiraj insisted on coming with me.

"You and Mummy have a lot of arguments, don't you?" he asked, when we'd crossed one street from our home.

I didn't answer and kept on walking, banging into a man carrying a bundle of fabric. He almost dropped it from his hand. "God has given you eyes as big as seashells; why don't you watch where you're going?" he sneered.

"Don't talk to my sister like that. If you didn't use your package as an eye patch you would've seen her coming," Chiraj said. The man gave us both a stern look and hurriedly walked away.

"Chiraj, I know you mean well. But just because you're a boy doesn't mean you have to take care of me. I can defend myself," I said.

"I know you can. Where do you think I learned to talk like that? From you. Remember how you told Mummy not to pressure Mohini into deciding who she wanted to marry? You always stood up for Mohini, so why can't I stand up for you?"

"Thanks," I mumbled, and walked quietly for a while. "Mummy and I disagree about many things. It's always been that way. You're older now, so maybe you notice more and think that I talk back to Mummy too much."

"It's not always your fault. I don't blame you."

Instead of being agitated about what Mummy had said to me, I wondered if Chiraj was worried. Did he suspect something was wrong between Anoop and Mohini? Did he wonder why she had come home so soon?

When Mohini returned from Nimita's house, we whispered until one of us fell asleep while listening to the other. Mummy slept in a far corner and couldn't hear what we were saying, but told us, "Stop *goos-poos* and go to sleep."

For the first few days after Mohini returned from America, she was happy to be back, but occasionally she wondered if coming back was the right thing to do. Wasn't an Indian girl supposed to stay with her husband no matter what? Wasn't running away from trouble the cowardly thing to do? I assured her that no one deserved to be abused. That in coming home she showed a lot more courage than if she had stayed with Anoop.

One night I told Mohini about Neel.

"Last year I wouldn't have approved of your seeing Neel, but I feel different now. You're lucky to have found someone so kind and smart. But if Mummy finds out about Neel she'll be hysterical."

"It'll be a nightmare from hell," I said. I tried to keep my voice calm, but my body turned as stiff as a bamboo pole.

"What will you do?"

"I'll still find a way to see him."

"I don't doubt that. You've always done what you thought was right."

"Shouldn't I?"

"You should. Because of what happened to me, I feel like I understand you more. Maybe I've changed."

"What do you mean?"

"Do you remember the time I wondered how Sarina could call light-skinned American girls her sisters? I asked you if they were from her caste or even Indian."

"Yes."

"Now it makes no difference to me. Karen helped me out so much that I shudder to think what would've happened to me without her. Besides you and Nimita, my own sisters, she's cared about me the most. We worked together for such a short time, and yet it didn't matter to her. I'll always think of her as my third sister."

"I'm so thankful she was there for you."

"Jeeta," she said, touching my shoulder, "without your support, I'd have never left Anoop. I would have worried about how Mummy would react and what people would say. Ever since we were little you've been the brave one. When I was afraid of Anoop, I thought about you and what you would do if you were in my place. I was surprised by my own courage. I didn't think I had any."

"You're back, and you can make things happen for you."

"Yes, now I can imagine a new life for me. I'll need that courage now more than ever to live a life that I want to live."

One day Mummy asked Mohini, "How long can you stay?"

"As long as she wants to," I replied.

"Are you still Mohini's lawyer?"

"She hasn't fired me." I glanced at Mohini. She was trying to smile but it wasn't working. "Mummy, after such a long journey, she is too tired to think about going back."

"I was just wondering."

I was glad she didn't pursue it further.

* * *

"In dealing with men, one must be extremely careful," Mummy said to me while I was washing mung beans one morning.

"Are you telling me this to prepare me for college?"

"I don't know what good it will do. You're as stubborn as a mule."

"Then you have nothing to worry about," I said as I sloshed the beans around in water. They looked like tiny marbles and made rattling sounds.

"Why not?"

"Because no one is going to like a mule."

"Tell me if I'm wrong, but it seems that my advice doesn't get through to you. You think I'm too old-fashioned. Listen to me now or cry later, because throughout the ages men have been the same. If they can get away with it, they'll take advantage of you. Don't be trapped by their sweet tongues. And stop playing with the mung beans. It's giving me an earache."

I rubbed the beans between my fingers one more time before I drained away all the water and filled the pan up with fresh water. I put the pan on the stove, covered it, wiped my hands, and offered Mummy these words: "Don't worry, I promise you, I won't show interest in any boys at my college."

She lapped up my syrupy words. "Good girl."

It rained only one day in May and then waited until June to strike again. College was starting the following week, so Sarina and I went shopping for our books. Luckily, the rain came right after we got to her house. Mumbai's rain always came at a slant, and even with umbrellas we got wet. We sat in the living room, watching the palm trees sway in the wind. Marine Drive changed its face, and the ocean looked like a naughty child dancing in the rain.

The funny thing about a monsoon storm is that how you feel about it depends entirely on whom you're with. When I watched the storm with Chiraj and Vivek, I felt cozy sitting on the bed playing cards. With Sarina I felt happy talking or studying. Listening to the rain alone, I felt like a lost ship on the ocean. I had never been in the rain with Neel, but I could imagine his arm around me, my heart pumping wildly as we watched the storm.

On Saturday I told Mummy I was going to Sarina's house, and when I got there Neel was waiting for me. He took me to a movie. While enjoying the movie, I didn't worry about anything, but when we got out of the Eros Theatre, it was still light outside, and I felt vaguely uncomfortable. Was someone watching me? I turned around and looked, but didn't recognize anyone. "Stop being nervous," Neel said, putting his hand on my shoulder.

But I still had a feeling that we were being watched. As I glanced over my shoulder this time, I saw a face disappear behind a pillar covered with movie posters. Was that Pankaj Kaka or someone else I knew?

"What's the fun of going out when you're so scared? Why not tell your family about us and be done with it," Neel said as we got to Marine Drive. The ocean was calm and there were many people strolling on the footpath.

"I can't."

"I met your mummy once. Can't you tell her I'm your friend?"

"You don't know Mummy. She'd boil like hot oil if she found out I'd gone to a movie with you."

"Since you and Sarina are taking different subjects, you won't even have an excuse to study with her."

"I know," I mumbled.

I knitted my fingers with his. We walked quietly. I wondered if our thoughts crossed without ever coming out of our heads. When we get to know someone well, do we speak silently?

"Did you enjoy the movie?" he asked.

"Yes, very much."

"And you enjoyed going out with me?"

"What do you think?"

"I think you did, and I'd like to take you out again."

"So you had a good time, too?"

"Tell me, when can we do this again? Next week?"

"I don't know."

He didn't say anything. He bought some peanuts from a vendor and we both ate as we strolled along the ocean. It wasn't raining, but the air was heavy and it felt as though we were waddling through it.

Then it was time for me to go home. I was afraid Neel would ask when I could see him again. I hated myself for not knowing the answer. Instead he asked, "Your mummy likes Sarina, right?"

"She likes her a lot."

"Then, if you tell her that Sarina and I are cousins, and the three of us are good friends, wouldn't she be fine with it? That way you can be honest with her and not have to make excuses to see me."

"I wish it were that simple. Think of the time when your grandmother was our age. Would her mother have allowed her to go out with a boy?"

"Of course not. Fifty years ago no one would have. But now it is different, isn't it?"

"Not for Mummy."

"What will you do if your mummy never lets you see me?"

"I'll see you somehow. You know that."

"I suppose," he said. His voice sounded dull, as if all the emotion had been sucked out of it.

By the time I got home I was mad at everyone: at Mummy for being so unreasonable, at Neel for insisting on my telling Mummy about us, and at myself for not having the courage to tell her.

seventeen

AS SOON AS I entered the house I found Mummy waiting for me in the living room. Even before I took my sandals off, she said, "Where have you been? And with whom? You think I don't know what you're doing? You're determined to spoil your reputation and drown our family name."

"What have I done?"

"Who is the *hali-mavali* people have seen you with? Who is he?"

He's not a hali-mavali; *he's a decent person,* I wanted to shout. Instead I stood there without answering. If Mummy didn't know much, then opening my mouth would just give her more information. The door to the bedroom was closed and I saw Mohini's and Chiraj's faces pressed against the iron grille of the window. Mummy had made them all go into the bedroom.

I stared at the picture of Krishna Bhagavan and begged for courage. He smiled back mysteriously.

My silence made Mummy angrier. "Three or four people have mentioned that they've seen you with a boy. Are they right?"

I stayed quiet.

"Why can't you be like Nimita and Mohini? Why do you have to run around with who knows what kind of boy? Answer me. Have you been going out without telling me? Have you?"

"Yes, but—"

"What's his name? Who's ruining your reputation and ours?"

"He is not, and—"

"Don't argue with me. Tell me his name."

"I can't tell."

"I'll not allow you to set foot outside the house until you tell me you won't see this boy anymore."

"He is a friend and I will see him."

"Look at your sisters. Haven't we found them good matches? Nimita and Girishji are so happy, and Mohini and Anoop—"

"Don't even mention Anoop. You don't know what he did to Mohini. He's not the son-in-law you think he is."

"What are you blathering about?"

"You think Mohini is back because she missed us and Anoop was nice to send her back! It's not true. She came without telling him. He hit her, Mummy, more than once, and so hard one time that she had to go to the hospital. She had to run away."

"You're lying."

"I am not a liar. Ask Mohini."

Mummy's face turned as pale as a lump of butter. She grabbed the edge of the divan. "Call her."

I opened the bedroom door.

"Mohini, is this . . . is this true?" Mummy could barely get the words out.

Mohini nodded.

Mummy collapsed on the divan. "He hit you? Where?"

"It doesn't matter. I'm fine now."

Tears rolled down Mummy's face as she held Mohini in her arms like she would never let her go.

After that Mummy didn't ask me about Neel. Her eyes bore the pain she felt for Mohini.

That night Mummy and Pappa talked late into the night. Even though I couldn't hear what they were saying, their voices flowed smoothly, and before long I fell asleep.

The next morning Pappa and I went to the Hanging Gardens for a walk. The entrance to the park was quiet, since we'd arrived earlier than the food vendors.

"Come, sit here," Pappa said, sitting on a bench. The air was scented with the ocean, the earth, and the fragrance of cannonball flowers. New leaves on the monkey topiary had burst forth, changing its shape. Everything was fresh, delicate, boundless.

A class of seven-year-olds passed by with their teacher. The girls wore white dresses with red belts, and the boys wore white shirts, khaki shorts, and red ties. "I can still picture you like this," sighed Pappa, pointing to the children.

I put my hand on his.

"Did Mummy talk to you last night?"

"Yes."

"I shouldn't have blurted out about Anoop."

"Sooner or later we had to tell Mummy."

Pappa always had a faraway look when he was deep in thought.

I dug my heels into the moist, red soil. "There is something I have to tell you."

"Yes?"

I summoned up my courage. "I want to tell you about someone."

"Then tell me."

I told him about Neel. He listened intently to all I had to say. I had no idea how he felt about it. Finally, when I told him that Neel was Sarina's cousin, he seemed to relax a bit.

"I'd like to meet him," he said.

I nodded.

At last, I felt free, like a cloud made light after a rainstorm.

Two weeks after college started, I was sitting on the divan reading my book when Mummy sat down on the chair across from me. I didn't look up. "Believe it or not, someone has approached me with your *manga*, a marriage offer," she said.

"I'm not interested."

"At least listen to me."

"Please, Mummy, I have too much studying to do."

"I told them you're too young."

"You said that?" I felt surprise all the way through my heartbeat.

"For now," she said. "You're not going to run away and get married?"

I looked in her eyes. "No, I'm not going to do that."

"Are you serious with that boy?" she said, fingering the page I was reading.

"Right now the only thing I'm serious about is this," I said, pointing at my book.

"You're young now, but remember, youth makes a bad friend. One day she is your best friend and the next day she leaves you forever. If you spend the next ten years studying, you might find yourself too old, and single. Then don't blame me."

"I won't." I was surprised how calm my voice was.

"They're still going to blame me. What am I to do?" She threw her hands in the air.

"Who's going to blame you?"

"Society, caste, neighbors."

"You can't put reins on their tongues," I said, and closed my book.

She said a few more things. I listened without saying a word. Frustrated with my silence, she left me alone and went to the bedroom.

I walked to the window. Four pigeons sat on the other side of the iron grille. They were so used to people that they didn't fly away. The sound that came out of their puffed-up throats was muffled, *ghoo, ghoo.* I wondered how many pigeons lived on that concrete ledge, hugging the window.

Then I closed my eyes and imagined the dark koyal flying from one mango tree to another, singing.

glossary

Aaa su bole che?: What are you saying?

amla: Indian gooseberry, Emblic myrobalans. It is used in Ayurvedic medicine.

apsara: a celestial dancer

bahu: daughter-in-law

Bapre: an exclamation of surprise

batata vada: potato balls

Bess chani-mani: Sit quietly.

beta: my child

Bhagvad Gita: a religious classic of Hinduism.
It is a part of the *Mahabharat*.

bhajans: devotional songs

Bharat Chhodo: Quit India movement of 1942 (*Bharat chhodo*) was a call for immediate independence of India from British rule issued by Mahatma Gandhi on August 8, 1942.

Bheem: one of the five brothers of the Pandava family from the *Mahabharat*, known for his appetite and strength *bhel-puri*: popular snack made of puffed rice, potatoes, savory noodles, *puris*, and various chutneys

bhine-vaan: wet complexion, dark

bhine-saan: soggy sensibility

bindi: a red or colored dot applied on the forehead

brahmi: leaves of the tree Bacopa monniera. It is used in Ayurvedic medicine

carrom: a board game played with *carrom* coins and a striker

chiki: peanut and brown sugar candy. It can also be made with other nuts or sesame seeds with brown sugar.

choop: quiet

Choop ker!: Be quiet!

Chut mangani, putt shadi: (Hindi) quick engagement, instant wedding

dal: spicy soup made of a variety of lentils

Damyanti: princess in the ancient Hindu story

dandia raas: a circle dance done with hand-painted sticks

Deekro, jivta pale ane muva bale: "A son takes care of you while you're alive and cremates you when you die."

desi: a fellow countryman, another Indian

dholak: a drum

dhosa: a thin crepe of lentil and rice

dhuk, dhuk, dhuk: Heartbeat sound

Diwali: a festival of lights celebrated all over India

dodh dyha: an overly wise person

dupatta: a long scarf worn over a long shirt and baggy pants

Ek ja de chingari, Mahanal: "Give me one light, the Great One."

Foi: in Gujarat, one's father's sister is called *Foi*

Fua: Foi's husband

gajra: a small flower garland for the hair

gammar: dull-witted

gappa: lie

garba: a popular folk dance of Gujarat

ghazals: Urdu poems

ghee: clarified butter with a nutty flavor

goos-poos: private talks

gotli: the soft, edible part inside the pit of a mango

Gujju: Gujarati person

gunder: Sticky semitransparent substance secreted by the trunks of acacia trees.

guruji: a great teacher

hali-mavali: a useless guy

idlis: steamed lentil and rice cakes

Ja, ja: Literally, "Go, go." Usually said to mean "Nonsense!" or "Unbelieveable!"

jamai: son-in-law

Janmabhoomi Pravasi: a Mumbai newspaper

kajal: a black paste applied to the eyes

kalash: a round top on the peak of the temple, usually made of gold

kathak: North Indian classical dance

Kem cho?: How are you?

khandvi: thin rolls of buttermilk and chickpea flour with spices

koyal: a black, robin-size bird with a very distinctive, sweet call

kulfi: a creamy, frozen, ice-cream-like dessert

Kunti: mother of five Pandava brothers in the *Mahabharat*

kurta-pajama: long shirt and loose pants, man's outfit

ladu: sweet balls made of flour, sugar, and ghee

lafra: affair, scandal

Limca: sweet-and-sour-lime flavored drink

Mahabharat: the longest poem in world literature. It is a tale of dynastic struggle between the hundred Kauravas and their cousins, the five Pandavas.

mandap: A canopy under which the Hindu marriage ceremony takes place. It represents the universe.

manga: a marriage proposal

mehndi: a plant whose leaves are dried and crushed and then used to decorate the hands and feet in intricate designs. It leaves a red color, which slowly washes away in a few days.

Modh Bania: a subcast of *Bania*. The pattern of social classes in Hinduism is called the "caste system." Usually Banias were merchants by profession

Namaste: greeting

Na-re na: absolutely not

Navratri: fall harvest festival celebrating the mother goddess

neelkamal: blue lotus. It is made up of two words. *Neel* means blue, *kamal* means lotus

neem: a tropical tree with medicinal uses

odhani: half sari

O mara bap: literally, "Oh my father!" Usually said in frustration

Ooi Ma: literally, "Oh mother!" Usually said to express pleasant surprise or sudden pain

pagel: crazy, crazy one

pani-puri: tiny, puffed round bread filled with spices and potatoes

pundit: learned man, astrologer, Hindu priest

puri: puffed, round whole-wheat bread that is deep fried

raatrani: night-blooming jasmine

raita: salad of various vegetables or fruits mixed with yogurt and spices

rassgulla: creamy white balls of cheese in light syrup

rotli: a whole-wheat bread cooked on a stove

sagdi: a coal-burning portable stove

Salli, tara tukede-tukda kari fanki daish: "I will cut you up in pieces and throw them away."

salwar khameez: a long shirt and baggy pants worn with a matching scarf called a *dupatta*

sambhar: South Indian lentil and vegetable soup that comes in countless varieties

saras: good

shanti: peace

shehanai: a brass musical instrument

sherwani: long coat worn by men

shiva-stotra: prayer to Lord Shiva

shrikhand: thickened yogurt dessert

swaha: (Sanskrit) to put offerings of rice etc. into the holy fire

tabla: type of drums

tambura: a one-string instrument

thaga-thiya: dillydally

thali: a stainless steel plate

tiffin: container with three or four tiers that stack on top of each other that is used to deliver home-cooked meals.

tiffinwallah: people who collect the tiffins from students' homes and deliver them at lunchtime

Vatnu vateser shu kam kere che?: "Why are you turning tiny talk into a twisty tale?"

vidai: the good-bye ceremony for a bride

Vrushchik: the zodiac sign of Scorpion. In Indian astrology, a name is given according to a child's moon sign.

Wah!: exclamation

wallah: One employed in a particular occupation or activity: *a kitchen wallah; rickshaw wallahs.*

author's note

Opera House Theater has not been in operation for the past few years. Also, the Vihar Lake is off limits for security reasons. Vihar Lake is one of the sources of water for Mumbai. I have fond memories of both these places and wanted to include them in the story.